WITHDRAWN

DEAD CITY

DEAD CITY

JAMES PONTI

ALADDIN

NEW YORK LONDON TORONTO SYDNEY NEW DELHI

ALADDIN

An imprint of Simon & Schuster Children's Publishing Division
1230 Avenue of the Americas, New York, NY 10020
First Aladdin hardcover edition October 2012
Copyright © 2012 by James Ponti
All rights reserved, including the right of reproduction in whole or in part in any form.
ALADDIN is a trademark of Simon & Schuster, Inc., and related logo is a registered trademark of Simon & Schuster, Inc.
For information about special discounts for bulk purchases, please contact Simon & Schuster Special Sales at 1-866-506-1949 or business@simonandschuster.com.
The Simon & Schuster Speakers Bureau can bring authors to your live event. For more information or to book an event, contact the Simon & Schuster Speakers Bureau at 1-866-248-3049 or visit our website at www.simonspeakers.com.
Designed by Lisa Vega
The text of this book was set in Adobe Garamond.
Manufactured in the United States of America 0812 FFG
10 9 8 7 6 5 4 3 2 1
Library of Congress Cataloging-in-Publication Data
Ponti, James.
Dead City / by James Ponti. — 1st Aladdin hardcover ed.
p. cm.
Summary: Seventh-grader Molly has always been an outsider, even at New York City's elite Metropolitan Institute of Science and Technology, but that changes when she is recruited to join the Omegas, a secret group that polices and protects zombies.
ISBN 978-1-4424-4129-3
[1. Zombies—Fiction. 2. Supernatural—Fiction. 3. Mothers and daughters—Fiction. 4. New York (N.Y.)—Fiction.] I. Title.
PZ7.P7726De 2012
[Fic—dc23]
2011048445
ISBN 978-1-4424-4128-6 (eBook)

For Denise:
wife, muse, and all-around cool chick

Acknowledgments

Only one name goes on the title page, but so many people go into bringing a book to life. I am beyond grateful for the entire Aladdin team, who did everything from undangling my modifiers to designing the look of the book. Triple thanks to my guardian angels, Fiona Simpson and Bethany Buck. If I had an Omega Team of my own, you'd be the first two I'd pick.

I leaned heavily on a small circle of dedicated readers who offered encouragement and suggestions along the way. This was especially true of Kim, Kim, Wyatt, and Adam. I'm leaving off your last names because I don't want any other writers to steal you. And I leaned even more heavily on my amazing literary agent, Rosemary Stimola. In addition to being accomplished in three separate careers, you're quite the amateur psychologist, strategic planner, and friend.

And finally, while all of the undead characters in this book are fictional, there were many sleep-deprived nights when I began to exhibit the traits of the worst Level 3 zombies. I cannot say enough about my wife and kids for putting up with it all. You amaze me every day.

You're Probably Wondering Why There's a Dead Body in the Bathroom . . .

I hate zombies.

I know that sounds prejudiced. I'm sure some zombies are really nice to kittens and love their parents. But it's been my experience that most are not the kind of people you want sending you friend requests.

Consider my current situation. Instead of eating pizza with my teammates as they celebrate my surprise victory at the St. Andrew's Prep fencing tournament, I'm trapped in a locker-room toilet stall.

With a dead body.

It's not exactly the Saturday I had planned. I wasn't

even supposed to compete in the tournament. Since most of the girls on the team are juniors and seniors and I'm in seventh grade, I was just going to be an alternate. But Hannah Gilbert didn't show up, and I filled in for her at the last moment. Five matches later my teammates were jumping up and down and pouring Gatorade on my head.

And that was the first problem.

I may not be the girliest girl, but I didn't really want to ride the subway with sticky orange hair. So I decided to clean up while everyone else headed down to the pizzeria to get a table and order a couple of large pies.

I had just finished my shower when I heard zombie noises coming my way. (I know, they hate to be called the z-word, but I hate being attacked in the bathroom, so I guess we're even.)

At first I thought it was one of my teammates playing a joke on me. But when I saw the reflection of the walking dead guy in the mirror, I realized it was Life playing a joke on me. I mean, is it too much to ask for just a couple hours of normal?

To make matters worse, this zombie and I had something of a history. During an earlier encounter, I sort of chopped off his left hand. I won't go into the details, but trust me when I say it was a "have to" situation. Anyway, now he was looking to settle a grudge, and all my gear was in a bag on the other side of the locker room. Too bad, because moments like these were the reason I took up fencing in the first place.

He looked at me with his cold dead eyes and waved his stump in my face to remind me why he was in such a bad mood. All I had to protect myself with was the towel I was wearing and my flat iron. Since I was not about to let Mr. Evil Dead see me naked, I went with the flat iron.

My first move was to slash him across the face, which was a total waste of time. Yes, it burned a lot of flesh. But since zombies feel no pain, it didn't slow him down one bit. Plus, no way was I ever going to let that flat iron touch my hair again, so I was down thirty bucks and I still had a zombie problem.

Next, he slammed me against the wall. That hurt unbelievably bad and turned my shoulder purple. (A color I like in clothes, but not so much when it comes to skin tone.) On the bright side, when I got back up I was in the perfect position for a *ballestra*, my favorite fencing move. It combines a jump forward with a lunge, and it worked like a charm.

The flat iron punctured his rib cage and went deep into his chest. It got stuck when I tried to yank it out, so I just started flicking it open and shut inside his body. This distracted him long enough for me to grab him at the base of the skull and slam his head into the marble countertop.

I don't know how much tuition runs at St. Andrew's, but their bathrooms have some high-quality marble. He went from undead to just plain dead on the spot.

All told, it took about forty seconds. But that's the problem with killing zombies. It's like when my dad and I make spaghetti sauce together. The hard part's not so much the doing as it is the cleanup afterward.

If this had been a public-school locker room, there would have been some gray jumbo-sized garbage cans nearby, and I probably could've taken care of cleanup by myself. But apparently the girls of St. Andrew's don't throw anything away, because all they had was a tiny wastebasket and some recycling bins. There were bins for paper, plastic, and glass, but none for rotting corpses. Go figure.

That meant I had to drag the body into a stall, text my friends for help, and call my coach with an excuse about how I had to go straight home. Now I'm stuck here sitting on a toilet, my hair's a total mess, and after two bottles of hand sanitizer, I still feel like I've got dead guy all over me. And don't even get me started about how hungry I am!

If you had told me any of this a few months ago, I

would have said you needed to visit the school nurse. That's because before I was Molly Bigelow, superhero zombie terminator, I was just an invisible girl in the back of the classroom who you'd probably never notice.

I'm sure none of this makes any sense. I mean, it's still hard for me to understand, and I'm the one who just did it. So while I wait for help to arrive, I'll try to explain. I understand if you don't believe it, but trust me when I say that every word is true.

It all started more than a hundred years ago, when an explosion killed thirteen men digging one of New York's first subway tunnels. But my part didn't begin until one day last summer, when I was hanging out at the morgue. . . .

Ω

Ω **1**

That Weird Bigelow Girl

I t was the last Friday of summer vacation, and I was running late. I'd made it halfway out the front door when I heard my dad call out from the kitchen.

"Molly, you forgot something."

"I took the trash out last night," I answered.

"Not the trash."

I started to run through a quick mental list of my chores. "I've got my lunch right here," I said, holding up my brown bag.

"Not your lunch."

I rolled my eyes and walked back to the kitchen doorway to look at him. He'd worked the late shift and was still wearing his navy blue paramedic's uniform as he hunched over a bowl of cereal.

"You want to give me a hint?"

He smiled that goofy dad smile and raised his cheek up to be kissed.

"Seriously?"

"What?" he answered. "You're worried someone might see you in our apartment? Worried that it could ruin your reputation?"

"It's not that. It's just that I'm not a little kid," I explained. "I don't need a kiss every time I go outside."

"Notice the cheek," he said, tapping it for emphasis. "I get the kiss, not you."

It was pointless to argue, so I walked over and gave him a peck on the cheek. As I did, he turned his head and gave me one too.

"Gotcha," he said with a movie villain's laugh. "By the way, last night I used those same lips to give mouth-to-mouth resuscitation to this really old woman. She was scary looking and had bad breath. She even had a little mustache thing going on." He added a couple of hacking coughs. "I hope I didn't catch something."

"You see what I mean?" I said with exasperation. "Nothing in my life can be normal."

"Normal?" He laughed. "Aren't you the girl on her way to hang out . . . at the morgue?"

I tried to give him my scrunched-up angry face, but I couldn't help laughing. He kind of had a point, so I rewarded him with an unsolicited good-bye hug.

He smiled. "Was that so hard?"

"Can I go now?"

"You can go. Say hi to Dr. H for me."

"I will," I answered as I hurried out the door and down the hall.

I do realize that it's not normal for a girl my age to hang out at the morgue. (Okay, I realize that it's not normal for a girl of *any* age to hang out at the morgue.) But I guess the first thing you should know about me is that I'm not exactly a cookie-cutter kind of girl. Even if I wanted to be, I think my mother had other plans.

When I begged her to put me in ballet class, she somehow convinced me that Jeet Kune Do was a better fit. So after school on Tuesdays and Thursdays, when the rest of the girls were learning *pirouettes* and *grand jetés*, I was down the hall mastering the martial art of the intercepting fist.

11

And when I wanted to join the Brownies, she signed me up for the New York City Audubon Society's Junior Birder program instead. As a result, I don't know a thing about cookies or camping but can identify sixty-eight different varieties of birds known to inhabit the five boroughs.

She even led me to the morgue.

My mom was a forensic pathologist for the New York City Office of Chief Medical Examiner. When the police needed help figuring out precisely how somebody died, they called her. She was really good at her job. The best. Sometimes she was even on TV or in the newspaper when she had to testify at a murder trial.

I know it sounds gory and gross, but she loved it. She liked to say that "even after someone dies, they still have a story to tell."

One Friday when I was seven years old, my grandma was supposed to watch me. At the last minute she couldn't make it, and Mom had no choice but to take me to work with her.

I can still remember how terrified I was as we rode the subway into the city. I'd always pictured her office looking like something out of a horror movie, with dead bodies scattered all over the place. But it wasn't like that at all. It turned out to be the most amazing science lab I could have ever imagined. I liked everything about it, except for the dead bodies. But they were mostly kept out of the way.

Going to the morgue became our thing to do. During the summers I went to work with her every Friday. She was careful not to let me see anything too gross, because she didn't want to give me nightmares. But she taught me all kinds of experiments and showed me how to use the cool equipment. Eventually, I even got less and less freaked out by the dead people.

"Death is part of the natural order of life," she would explain. "You shouldn't be scared of it. You should be respectful of it."

A couple of years later, when they diagnosed her cancer and she started going to chemotherapy, she used the morgue to help prepare me, in case she died. She explained that while the human body was amazing, it had limitations. She wanted me to know that when her body gave out, her spirit and soul would still live on in me and my sister.

Mom died two summers ago. It was a Sunday morning, and I remember every single thing about that day. I remember the smell of the pretzels for sale outside the hospital and the mechanical sounds of the monitors in her room. I remember that everything about her looked pale and weak and unrecognizable—except her eyes.

My mom had mismatched eyes. It's called "hetero-chromia," and I have it too. My left eye is blue and my right is green, just like hers. She said it was our special genetic bond.

That day, I looked deep into her eyes. Everything else was failing, but they still looked as sharp and bright as ever.

"Even after someone dies . . . ," she whispered.

"They still have a story to tell," I finished.

She smiled and then added, "That's right, and my story is going to be told by you."

I was amazed by how many people came to her funeral. The policemen who worked with her on cases and the paramedics and firemen from my dad's station house were all there wearing their dress uniforms. They looked so big and strong. And every one of them cried.

Everyone cried that day . . . but me.

The following Friday, I rode the subway into the city and went to her office like I always had. I don't really know what I was thinking or expecting. It was just a habit. But nobody said anything about it or asked me why I was there. They just acted like I belonged.

That day I hung out with Dr. Hidalgo, my mom's best friend. I've been going back and hanging out in his office on summer Fridays ever since. And because this was the last Friday of summer vacation, I didn't want to be late.

"Waiiiit!" I yelled as I raced down the hall.

I sprinted the last few strides and managed to jam my hand inside the elevator just as the door was closing. When it sprang back open to reveal who was riding it, I wished that I had just slowed down and waited for the next one.

There was Mrs. Papadakis, whose two favorite hobbies are gossiping and tanning. Judging by her bathing suit, which was inappropriate by at least thirty years and sixty pounds, she was on her way to the courtyard to do both with a group of old ladies I call the Leather Bags. You always have to be careful about what you say or do around her, because anything slightly embarrassing is bound to be the talk of the building by the end of the day.

Next to her were Dena and Dana Salinger, twin sisters from down the hall who like to do everything together—especially torment me. One time they pinned me in the elevator and forced me to ride all the way to the fifteenth floor. They pushed me out into the hallway, even though they knew I was terrified of heights and never went above the third floor.

Today they wore leopard-print bikini tops and matching short shorts and were headed to Astoria Park, a huge public pool just down the street from our apartment building.

But the person I dreaded most was the girl with the Salingers. The one who was giving me the stink eye.

It was my sister, Beth.

Normally, Beth and I have an "ignorance is bliss" policy when we cross paths away from home. She ignores me and I'm blissful about it. It's not that we don't love each other. It's just I'm in middle school, and she's in high school. I'm brainy and nerdy, and she's cool and popular. But as I stepped into the elevator, I was pretty sure she was going to say something.

"What do you think you're doing with that jacket?" she demanded.

Did I forget to mention that while everyone else looked like they stepped out of the swimsuit edition of *Queens Apartment Living*, I was wearing jeans, a long-sleeved T-shirt, and, most important to Beth, carrying a bright pink ski parka.

"You know," she continued, "the jacket that belongs in *my* closet."

Bank vaults had nothing on my sister when it came to protecting her clothes. That's the reason I was running late. I'd waited inside the apartment for nearly forty minutes after she'd left, just to avoid the possibility of bumping into her. Now I was stuck with her on the world's slowest elevator. Apparently, it had taken the Salingers longer than usual to spray on their fake tans.

"It's Friday," I explained. "You know how cold it gets in the morgue."

"The morgue?" Mrs. Papadakis screeched, her Queens accent exaggerating the word. "Did somebody die?"

"No," I answered sheepishly.

"Then why are you going to the morgue?"

I didn't know what to say, so I just told the truth. "I like to hang out there."

Beth cringed. It was bad enough that her little sister was "that weird Bigelow girl from the third floor." She didn't need everyone to know how weird I really was.

"You hang out at a morgue?" Dana said.

"Your sister is a *total* freak, Beth," Dena added.

Beth shot them a look that seemed almost protective of me. But then she gave me one that was even angrier. "What's wrong with *your* jacket?"

"I got cadaver juice on it last week," I said as though that was a normal conversation topic. "I've washed it seven times, but it still stinks."

Mrs. Papadakis almost threw up at the mention of "cadaver juice."

"So your brilliant idea was to get some on mine?"

"No. I won't. I promise. Dr. H isn't even doing an autopsy today. I called and checked."

"It doesn't matter what Dr. H is or isn't doing," she said, "because you are going upstairs and putting it back in my closet where you found it."

"If I don't have a jacket, it'll be too cold in the morgue," I pleaded.

She gave me that "condescending older sister" look. "Then I guess you won't go."

I thought about it for a moment before I flashed my "evil little sister" smirk and then said, "Okay. I guess I won't. Maybe I'll go swimming at Astoria Park instead. I can work on my butterfly stroke. It's kind of awkward, and I splash a lot, but who cares if people stare. Besides, I can always ask for help. You know, from the boys you'll be flirting with. Then the four of us girls can hang out."

Both Salingers shot Beth a look, and I knew I had won.

"Fine," Beth said curtly. "You can borrow it. But if you get so much as a drop of water on it, you're buying me a new one."

"Deal," I said as we stepped into the lobby.

I only made it a few steps before Mrs. Papadakis decided she just had to butt in. She put a caring hand on my shoulder, like we had some sort of close relationship . . . which we don't.

"Darling, it is not appropriate for a girl your age to visit the morgue. I know your mother—"

The mention of my mother was as far as she got.

Beth literally stepped between us and said, "Mrs. Papadakis, my mother thought you were a joke. I'm sure she wouldn't want either one of us to take advice from you. So save yourself the trouble."

Mrs. Papadakis's eyes opened wide. "Well, aren't you so very rude?"

"Really?" Beth said, not backing down. "Because I thought it wasn't nearly as rude as a woman your age trying to bully my little sister into feeling bad about herself."

Did I forget to mention that despite our many differences, my sister totally rocks?

Popsicles and Vanilla

Mornin', Molly," the security guard said as I entered the lobby of the morgue. Jamaican Bob was tall and thin and wore his dreadlocks pulled back in a ponytail. "You know, it's a good thing you got here when you did," he continued. "The building's going to be jam-packed today."

"Why is that?" I asked as I emptied my pockets into a plastic tray and walked through the metal detector.

"Haven't you heard about the morgue?" he said with a booming laugh. "Everybody's *dying* to get in."

Bob always told the corniest jokes, but I had to laugh because he got such a kick out of them.

"Have a good day," I said as I took my backpack from the X-ray machine.

"I will," he answered with a big smile. "As long as I stay up here and away from that freezer of yours."

Like a lot of the people in the building, Bob was freaked out by the freezer, which is what we called the body storage area, located three floors underground.

I guess it takes a while to get used to the idea of being surrounded by dead bodies.

Even when you do get used to it, there are two things you need to bring with you whenever you work in the morgue. The first is a jacket, because the bodies are refrigerated well below freezing. (If yours is not available, you can always steal your sister's.)

The second is vanilla extract to fight the smell. My mom taught me this trick the first time I went to work with her. Now I always bring a bottle with me when I come to the morgue. I swipe a finger of it under my nose every hour or so. (Unfortunate side effect: Vanilla milk shakes now make me think of dead people.)

"Somebody got a new jacket," Natalie said when I entered the lab.

"That's because somebody spilled cadaver juice on my other one," I reminded her.

"Oh yeah," she answered with a sheepish grin. "Sorry about that."

"I had to steal this one from my sister's closet," I explained. "If anything gets on it, I'm going to end up with the Popsicles." (That's what we call the dead bodies.)

Natalie is Dr. Hidalgo's intern. Like me, she's a student at MIST—the Metropolitan Institute of Science and Technology, a science magnet school that draws kids from all over New York City.

MIST is made up of two separate schools. The Lower School is for sixth, seventh, and eighth grades, while the Upper School is for ninth through twelfth. I'm in the Lower School and Natalie's in the Upper. Normally, high schoolers don't mingle with Lowbies, but since Nat and I were often the only living people in the room, we had gotten to know each other pretty well during the summer.

Natalie talks like a total science geek but looks like she belongs on the cover of a fashion magazine. Not only does she discuss everything from DNA sequencing to nanotechnology, but she does it with perfect hair, flawless skin, and the cutest clothes you ever saw.

Our backgrounds are different in nearly every way. Natalie lives on the Upper West Side. She never flaunts it, but you can tell her family has serious money, with doormen in the lobby and park views from the terrace. Her parents are both surgeons, and everything about their life has a feeling of fabulous about it. She even owns a horse named Copernicus that she rides some weekends.

Despite our differences, we'd become real friends over the summer. Or at least I hoped we had. I've never been great at judging social situations. I wondered if the friendship would continue back at school or if it was just convenient since we're both at the morgue.

"What's on the schedule for our last day?" I asked.

"A surprise," answered a voice from behind me.

I turned to see Dr. Hidalgo entering the room.

"We're going on a field trip," he continued, heading to his desk and grabbing his medical bag.

Natalie and I gave each other a "did he just say what I think he said" look. We never left the lab. *Never.* A field trip could mean only one thing.

"To a crime scene?" she asked, trying to mask her obvious excitement. "We're going to a crime scene?"

"Yes." He took a camera from a shelf and then slipped it into his bag. "We are going to a crime scene."

"And you're cool with us being there?" I asked. "Nightmare-wise?"

"I give you my no-nightmares guarantee," he assured

us as he held three fingers in the air like a Boy Scout taking an oath.

A few things you should know about Dr. H. First of all, he's awesome. He's been like family my whole life. Second, he has obsessive-compulsive disorder and is the neatest, most organized person I have ever met. He has wire-rimmed glasses and always wears a bow tie that matches his socks. He keeps his nails perfectly manicured and gets the same haircut from the same barber every other Thursday.

He has a way to do things, and that's the way he always does them. My mom once told me that's why he's such a brilliant medical examiner. He's so obsessive that he notices when any detail is out of place.

One example of his OCD is that whenever he leaves for a crime scene, he follows the exact same routine. First, he pulls a new legal pad from the supply cabinet and writes the case number, time, and location across the top three lines.

Next, he calls the staff secretary and gives her the same information, so that she can open an official file. Finally, he grabs his doctor's bag and the keys to Coroner's Van #3 and drives to the crime scene. He says he likes #3 because it has the best radio.

This time, however, he didn't do any of those things. He just rushed out the door.

"It will be quicker if we walk," he explained as we scrambled to stay with him in the maze of hallways that snake through the basement. "I know a shortcut."

I thought I knew my way around the morgue pretty well, but I was ready to start leaving bread crumbs so we could find our way back, when he suddenly popped open a door and we stepped out onto First Avenue. I had no idea how we got there, but I couldn't help noticing that his shortcut let us leave the building without anyone else knowing.

Dr. H didn't say anything about where we were going or what type of crime scene to expect. He just did his speed-walking thing while we tried to keep up. He spent most of the walk on the phone, arranging for someone to meet us. "This is it," he announced as he came to a stop in front of an alley on Second Avenue.

If this was a crime scene, I was underwhelmed. There were no detectives looking for clues. There was no mob of people trying to figure out what had happened. There wasn't even any of that yellow police tape. There was only a tall iron gate blocking off the alley.

"Someone should be here any minute to let us in," he continued.

The sign at the top of the gate read NEW YORK MARBLE CEMETERY. INCORPORATED 1831.

Just then, Natalie noticed something stuck between the edge of the sign and the top of the gate. "What's that?" she asked, pointing at it.

The sun was directly above us, so when we looked up, it was impossible to see clearly.

"Let's find out," Dr. H replied.

He grabbed a silver pointer from his bag, extending it until it was long enough to reach the sign. Then he put his arm through the bars and tapped at the object from behind so that it fell on our side of the gate.

"Got it," I said as I went to catch it.

"You might not want—" was all he got out before it was too late.

I caught it, and when I looked down, I realized it was a severed human finger. So much for the no-nightmares guarantee.

". . . to touch that," he said, completing his sentence.

I tried not to gag as I hot-potatoed it over to him.

"Impressive catch, though," he added. "Especially with the sun in your eyes."

Without missing a beat, Natalie grabbed a bottle of hand sanitizer from her backpack and gave it to me.

"Thanks."

"Left hand, ring finger," Dr. Hidalgo concluded instantly.

I was impressed. "You can tell that without the other fingers to go by?"

He held it up for us to see. "The wedding ring kind of helps."

Sure enough, there was a gold band around the base of the finger. I stared at the finger for a moment. Something about it seemed wrong. Then I realized what it was. There was no blood.

Dr. Hidalgo slipped the ring off the finger and checked the inside for an inscription. "*Amor Fidelis*, Cornelius," he read aloud. "Faithful love . . . Cornelius. Not a name you hear every day."

Once again, Dr. Hidalgo broke standard procedure. Rather than putting the finger into an official evidence bag and then labeling it, he slipped it and the ring into a plain plastic baggie and then dropped it into his doctor's bag.

A few minutes later, the caretaker of the cemetery arrived to unlock the gate for us. He told us he had to rush back to the office and asked Dr. Hidalgo if he could lock up when we left.

That meant we were all alone.

The cemetery looked like a small park. A tall stone wall wrapped around the edge. The only way in or out was through the gated alley.

"Look for anything out of the ordinary," Dr. H said as we began to spread out and scour the grounds.

"How's this for out of the ordinary?" I offered. "This cemetery doesn't seem to have any tombstones or graves."

"That's because a law was passed in the early 1800s that banned earthen graves in Manhattan," he explained. "The fear was that yellow fever would pass from the dead bodies into the soil and make its way back among the living."

"Then where are the bodies?" Natalie asked.

"They're in underground death chambers," he said.

"Death what?" I asked as I stopped in my tracks and processed yet another image for my sleepless nights.

"Marble rooms where they could place the corpses underground without having to worry about their decay contaminating the soil. Think of them as studio apartments for the afterlife. There's another cemetery just like it around the corner."

"And how is this a crime scene?" Natalie asked.

"Last night the police received a dozen phone calls complaining about loud noises coming from here."

"The crime is *loud noises*?" I asked.

"You saw how hard it was to get in." He motioned back to the alley. "Those gates are unlocked only one Sunday a month. Don't you wonder what was causing all the commotion?"

"Not particularly," I answered, getting a little spooked. Severed fingers, death chambers, and scary noises. As far as field trips went, this rated well below the Museum of Natural History. (But it was still better than our class visit to the wastewater treatment plant.)

"This is where the death house was," said Dr. H, coming to a stop. "A shed where the bodies were stored until they were buried. Kind of like the nineteenth-century version of our freezer at work."

"And you know all of this because . . . ?" I asked.

"Are you kidding?" he replied. "I'm a New York City medical examiner. I learn this stuff for fun."

Natalie and I both laughed, which made Dr. H laugh too. Then he noticed something.

"Check this out," he said, kneeling down.

A large square of grass looked like it had been pulled up and laid back down. It didn't stand out from a distance, but up close it was impossible to miss.

Dr. Hidalgo snapped a picture. Then he peeled back the corner of the grass to reveal a large stone slab. "It's a fieldstone cap," he said as he took another photograph. "Someone must have gone down into this entry shaft to reach one of the vaults."

I began to get a sinking feeling that he was expecting us to do the same.

"Look at this," he said with a smile. "They were in a hurry and didn't put the cap all the way back. We can slide it open."

"Lucky us," I said, trying to force a laugh.

Dr. H sat down, ignoring the threat of grass stains on his perfectly pressed pants, wedged himself into the ground, and started pushing the slab with his feet. It was a strain, but after a minute or so, he managed to move it far enough to reveal a dark shaft in the ground.

"You're not going down there, are you?" I asked.

"No," he said, to my momentary relief. "I'm much too big to fit in there. It's going to have to be one of you two."

"Seriously?" I said. "What about your no-nightmares guarantee?"

"I'll go, Dr. H," Natalie volunteered. "Molly's too scared to do something like that."

Instead of feeling relieved, I felt challenged. "I didn't say anything about being scared," I corrected. "Just let me think about it for a second."

I sat on the edge of the shaft and dangled my legs through the opening. "Okay, now I've thought about it. I'm in."

Dr. H and Natalie shared a smile.

"I'm very proud of you," he said as he handed me a small flashlight.

Natalie reached into her backpack again and pulled out the hand sanitizer. "I'm ready the moment you get back."

I gave her my sister's jacket. "Protect this with your life. If I take it down there, I might as well just stay in the vault."

A small ladder was built into the wall. I slowly climbed down into the shaft. Actually, I tried to do it slowly, but I lost my grip and fell into the darkness. I landed on my butt, and when I looked back up at them, the sunlight around their heads looked like halos.

"Are you okay?" Dr. H asked.

"I found the floor," I answered.

"There should be a door to the vault just to your left," Dr. H told me.

"I really can't believe I'm doing this," I said as I stood up and brushed the dirt off my hands. I pushed on the door and was surprised by how easily it swung open. The sunlight didn't quite reach here, so the vault was just empty darkness. It had a disgusting smell that made me wish I'd brought along my vanilla extract.

"What do you see?" Dr. Hidalgo asked.

"Nothing yet," I answered as I turned on the flashlight.

The shaft of light cut through the darkness. I knew that if I could do this, I could overcome almost any fear. I stepped all the way into the vault and looked around.

Thirty seconds later I stepped back out into the shaft and looked up at their still-haloed faces.

"Well?" Natalie asked nervously. "What did you see?"

"It's what I didn't see that's interesting," I replied. "Shouldn't there be dead people in there?"

3

The Reason I Hate Swans

After taking a deep breath and realizing that despite my worst fears, I was not going to uncover a pile of maggot-riddled corpses, I took Dr. Hidalgo's camera and went back into the burial vault for a second, slightly longer, look around. I counted enough slabs to hold ten bodies; each one was empty. Still, the vault rated pretty high on the creep-o-meter, so I took a few quick pictures and then climbed back up to the surface.

While the doctor scribbled some notes and I put the hand sanitizer to good use, Natalie went over to the wall where there are plaques that correspond with each of the vaults.

"According to this, there should be eight people buried in there," she said, reading from one. "All from the Blackwell family."

Dr. H nodded and wrote this down on his pad. "The Blackwells were an important family in the early history of New York," he said. "In fact, Blackwell's Island was the original name of Roosevelt Island."

Natalie and I shared a smile at the mention of Roosevelt Island. It's a thin strip of land in the East River that runs alongside midtown Manhattan. Hardly anyone lives on it and nothing much happens there, so most people never give it a thought. Natalie and I smiled because Roosevelt Island is a big part of our everyday lives. It's where our school is located.

"By the way," Dr. H asked Natalie, "are any of the Blackwells that are supposed to be in the vault named Cornelius?"

Natalie laughed, but she stopped cold when she looked at the plaque. "Yes!"

"Interesting," he replied as he made a note.

Natalie and I were stunned.

"How can that be?" I asked.

Dr. H looked up from his pad and answered, "My

guess is grave robbery, but that's something for the police to figure out."

We looked around the cemetery for a little while longer, but found nothing else that seemed out of the ordinary. Since it was our last Friday of the summer, Dr. Hidalgo treated us to lunch at Carmine's, where we shared big bowls of pasta and laughed at the retelling of my descent into the Blackwell crypt.

Despite Dr. H's promises, I did have a couple of bad dreams. But over the next few days the worries that kept me up at night went from severed fingers and robbing graves to fitting in and making friends. The first day of school was looming, and even in a student body filled with science geeks, I wasn't particularly skilled at social situations.

Every year more than a thousand students from across New York's five boroughs apply to MIST.

Only seventy get in.

Applying never would have occurred to me if not for the fact that my mother was a MIST grad. She'd always talked about me maybe going there, and just filling out the application made me feel closer to her. Even though I'm a good student, I was totally shocked when I was accepted. So now, in addition to our mismatched eyes, MIST is something special that the two of us share. Sometimes during lunch I like to sneak into the library to look for pictures of her in old yearbooks.

The student body isn't the only thing that makes MIST unusual. The campus looks like something out of a horror movie. The school is made up of four buildings that originally housed a mental hospital in the late 1880s. (That little tidbit is left off the brochure.)

In other ways, though, MIST is just like every other school—filled with cliques and rivalries, which is why I had an uneasy feeling as I got ready that morning. I even ignored all scientific reasoning and brought along a good-luck charm: a necklace with a little horseshoe on it that I had found in my mom's old jewelry box.

The first few classes went fine, but the moment I'd been dreading was lunch. That's where my solo status was at its most glaring. Unlike most middle school girls, who traveled in packs and coordinated their lives and ward-robes with their BFFs, I tended to do things by myself. This hadn't always been the case. For one three-and-a-half week period, I was part of a group.

I'm embarrassed to admit how much I liked it.

It started last year, right around Thanksgiving. Every day at lunch I sat at a table with the same six girls. We were all new to the school and were pretty intimidated, so we found our strength in numbers.

One day one of the girls, Jessica, said that our group should have a name. I wasn't sure if she was joking or not, but some of the others agreed with her, and suddenly finding a name became a big deal. Everyone tried to come up with one that would fit us.

Surprisingly, *I* was the one who did. It was the holiday season, and I had Christmas carols in my head. I blurted out, "Seven swans a-swimming."

"I love it," Jessica announced. "We're the *Swans*."

Pretty soon the bell rang, and I didn't think any more about it. But the next day when we sat down, Jessica had a surprise for us. She opened her lunch box and pulled out seven silver swan charms. She gave us each one and told us we should keep them in our backpacks. They would mark our secret sisterhood.

For reasons that I still cannot fully understand, I thought this was the coolest thing ever. Suddenly I was part of something special. Something secret. Sometimes I'd walk into a classroom and see that another one of the girls had drawn a little swan in the corner of the chalkboard, and I'd smile. It was our code.

Everything was great until Olivia came along. She

wanted to join the group, which seemed easy enough. We all liked her and, after all, there were eight seats at each cafeteria table. No one would even have to move.

But that's not how Jessica saw it.

"It doesn't make sense," she said. "She'd make eight, and there are only seven swans. Eight would make us maids a-milking, and I am not a maid."

Seriously, that's what she said.

I told her that the song didn't really matter. I reminded her that *I* had been the one to make up the name in the first place. But her mind was set. Seven swans, not one more or one less.

My mistake was thinking that all swans were created equal. I didn't realize that some were more equal than others and that Jessica had become our leader. In a show of protest I reached into my backpack, pulled out my swan, and slapped it on the table. I thought five other girls would join me in pointing out how ridiculous this was and do the same.

No one did.

They just sat there and stared at me like I was the world's biggest traitor. Before I knew it, Olivia had my swan charm and was sitting at the table with the other girls while I was all alone in a corner of the cafeteria. I was living a reverse fairy tale. I'd gone from swan to ugly duckling.

At Christmas, Jessica even gave me a nickname. She started calling me Partridge. "Because in 'The Twelve Days of Christmas,' the partridge is the one that's all alone."

Nine months later, I still felt anxious as I walked past their table to my corner spot.

When I sat down, I noticed Jessica giving me her usual superior look. But then a funny thing happened. Her smirk became a look of surprise with maybe even a hint of jealousy mixed in. I turned to see what had caused this and was amazed to find Natalie and two of her friends standing by my table, holding their lunches.

"Mind if we join you?" she said.

Lunch is one of the rare times when Upper School and Lower School students are together in one place. Even so, they hardly ever mingle. A Lowbie sitting at a lunch table with high schoolers is practically unheard of.

"Not at all," I said with a smile as I looked back at Jessica.

Natalie sat down and did some quick introductions.

"Molly, meet Alex and Grayson. Guys, this is Molly Bigelow."

"Nice to meet you," Grayson said.

"We heard you like to hang out at the morgue," Alex added with a smile. I wasn't sure if he was teasing me, but at the moment, just knowing that it was killing Jessica was all that mattered. Suddenly, I thought of Jamaican Bob, the security guard with the bad jokes.

"Well, you know what they say about the morgue," I said as coolly as I could. "Everybody's dying to get in."

It took a moment, but they all actually laughed. Although I had never met Alex or Grayson, I knew both of them by reputation. Alex was a boy version of Natalie. He had supergeek brains in a quarterback's body, and I wondered if they might be boyfriend and girlfriend. Grayson, on the other hand, looked more like you'd expect a science geek to look. A ninth grader, he was known as the school's resident computer genius, which is saying something at a place like MIST.

When he sat down, the first thing he did was look at me and say, "You're heterochromatic."

"What?" I asked.

"Heterochromatic," he repeated. "It means your eyes are different colors."

"I know what it means," I said. "It's just kind of an odd way to start a conversation."

"Grayson doesn't have much of a social filter," Natalie warned. "You get used to it."

Alex, meanwhile, was busy pulling out an amazing array of food from what had to be the world's largest lunch box. He had two ham-and-turkey sandwiches, a bag of chips, string cheese, two bananas, a box of crackers, raisins, and a can of soda.

I don't know if I actually said "wow" out loud, but I certainly thought it.

"Oh yeah," Natalie added. "And Alex eats more than any three people you've ever met. Try not to stare, he's very sensitive about it."

"I am not," said Alex as he chewed off the end of the string cheese.

"You should be," Grayson interjected.

"Is that so?" Alex said with a laugh. "You think *my* eating habits are embarrassing. You won't eat any food that's white. As if color affected the taste."

Grayson slumped. "We just met her."

Alex ignored him and turned to me. "I'm not joking. He won't eat mayonnaise, milk, eggs, vanilla ice cream, sour cream . . . anything white."

"I eat bread," Grayson offered.

"Only if it's toasted."

Grayson laughed and then added, "It tastes better toasted."

"So, now you know a little something about us," Alex said. "Let's find out about you."

"I eat almost anything," I said. "Except I don't like pickles or peaches."

"Because they both start with the letter *p*?" Grayson asked hopefully.

"No," I answered. "Because I don't like how they taste."

"How very reasonable," Alex said.

The joking and friendly teasing continued throughout lunch. I have to say that this group was a lot more fun than the Swans. I couldn't quite figure out how the three of them became friends, but I could tell they really were.

I also couldn't help but feel a little self-conscious. Throughout lunch, they kept asking me questions like they were interviewing me for the school paper.

They asked me about my friends (what friends?) and my taste in music (anything with a girl who plays guitar). They even wanted to know about the Junior Birder program. Part of me liked the attention but another part was exhausted by how relentless it all was.

"What do you want to be when you grow up?" Grayson asked.

"A doctor."

"Why?" asked Alex.

"That's kind of personal, don't you think?"

"I don't know," he said. "Is it?"

"It is to me," I explained. "A few years ago my mother died from cancer. During those last six months, I spent a lot of time in hospital rooms watching doctors work."

"And now you want to be like them?" Grayson asked.

I looked him in the eye and shook my head. "Didn't you hear me? I said she died. I'm going to be *better* than them."

And with that both Grayson and Alex smiled, and the questions stopped.

Natalie gave them a look and said, "Didn't I tell you?"

They both nodded.

"Tell them what?" I asked.

"Just that you were cool and that we should get to know you," Alex said.

Okay, no one ever called me cool before.

"We're really glad to have met you," Grayson said.

"Definitely," added Alex. "We've got to go help set up for the assembly, but we'll see you around. I promise."

They got up and left me alone with Natalie.

Once they were gone, I asked, "You want to explain what that was all about?"

"They're just a couple of friends of mine," she said. "I'd been talking about getting to know you over the summer, and they wanted to meet you. Don't worry. They're good guys."

Then something caught her eye. She leaned over and looked at my necklace. "Where'd you get that?"

"I found it in my mom's old jewelry box," I said. "Why?"

She looked a little concerned and then seemed to force a smile. "No reason. I just didn't remember your wearing it this summer."

"Yeah," I replied. "I thought a horseshoe might bring me some luck."

She nodded. "Let's hope so."

After lunch everybody went to the auditorium for the start-of-the-school-year assembly. As always, it began with an inspirational speech from our principal, Dr. Gootman.

"Immortality," he intoned as he gripped the podium. "The pursuit of science is the quest to render obsolete the boundaries of our mortal beings. It is the search for immortality." (No one talks like this, right? But Dr. Gootman really pulls it off.)

"Although scientific advancements have dramatically increased our lifespan, death is still inevitable. You cannot live forever." He took a long dramatic pause before adding, "Or can you?"

He held up a test tube so that it shimmered in the light. "This vial contains a strain of the bacterium *Saccharomyces cerevisiae*."

A girl sitting next to me gulped like it was some deadly form of anthrax.

"It's more commonly known as yeast," he continued, much to the girl's relief. "And as long as yeast is fed a steady diet of flour and water, it will live forever.

"This particular strain was created here at MIST as part of a chemistry experiment . . . in 1904."

He let the words sink in.

"Today we will do what has been done on the first day of each fall semester since then. We will eat bread made from this yeast. In doing so we will continue a meal that has included every student and teacher in this school's history."

He stopped and looked at the test tube for a moment. There was a touch of emotion in his voice as he continued. "The students from that chemistry class died long ago. But more than a century later, their experiment still thrives. Immortality.

"At most schools the mascot is some sort of cartoon animal—a ram or a bear on a football helmet. Welcome to the only school whose mascot is a single-celled bacterium. Welcome to MIST."

Why I Floss on a Daily Basis

Before I go any further, I should probably explain my intense fear of heights. It started with the scariest moment in my life. One evening when I was five years old, my mom and I had just left a movie theater and were walking down the street when a lunatic charged up to us and grabbed her purse. They had a quick tug-of-war, and when the purse strap broke, he fell to the ground. In a flash, my mom swooped me up into her arms and started running. Even though he had the purse, he still chased after us.

I was crying my eyes out, but Mom stayed cool and calm. She was concerned, but she was in control. First she ran into a building that was brightly lit. When he continued toward the building, she started to run up the stairs. I can still remember the sound of his shoes echoing in the stairwell as he ran up after us. Because I was facing back over her shoulder, I got a good look at his face.

I will never forget that face.

When we got to the top of the stairs, we burst through a door and onto the roof. My mom was still cool and calm. She set me down and picked up a brick. At first I thought she was going to use it to hit him when he came through the door. Instead, she used it to smash the door handle, breaking it so it wouldn't work.

Seconds later we could hear him pounding on the other side of the door. Her trick worked, and he couldn't get it to open. Eventually, he went away.

We were no longer in danger from the lunatic, but we had another problem. My mom had done such a good job of breaking the door, *we* couldn't open it either. And since her phone was in the purse that was stolen, we couldn't call anyone for help. We wound up stuck on the roof for the entire night. It was cold and rainy, and I was terrified. I was scared that if I fell asleep, I would somehow fall off the top of the building. Ever since, I've tried to avoid anything higher than our third-floor apartment.

This is why I've spent my entire life in New York without ever stepping foot in the Empire State Building or the Statue of Liberty. And it's why, when the assembly ended and school let out, I wasn't one of the kids headed for the Roosevelt Island tram.

The tram is the most popular way for people to get on and off the island. Up to a hundred and twenty-five people at a time get into the tram car (I like to call it the death cage) and take the four-minute ride over the East River. My problem is that along the way, the tram dangles from a cable about two hundred and fifty feet in the air.

I get ticked when people say I have a phobia. Phobias are based on irrational fears. My fear is rooted in a true scientific understanding of gravity. That's a big tram and that's a big drop.

Luckily, Roosevelt Island also has a subway station. It's not very busy, but the F train runs through it on the way to Queens, so it works perfectly for me. Well, it would be perfect if it weren't for the escalators.

Roosevelt Island Station is the second deepest in the entire subway system. It's like an upside-down ten-story building, and you have to ride a trio of unbelievably steep escalators to get down there. It's not the ideal thing for someone terrified of heights, but still *way* better than the tram.

That day, like most others, my solution for dealing with the escalator was to grab the handrail as tightly as I could and close my eyes until I reached the bottom.

If my eyes had been open, I might have seen the creepy guy a little bit sooner. Instead, I didn't notice him until after I had just missed the train and plopped down onto a bench to wait for the next one.

Or, put another way, I didn't realize he was there until I was completely alone and unprotected in a subway station one hundred feet below ground.

Once the rush of the departing train died down, the station fell virtually silent. The only noises were the buzzing of the lights hanging from the ceiling and the occasional crackle of electricity along the train's third rail.

Looking around, I noticed this guy sitting on another bench, staring right at me.

He was tall like a basketball player, and superthin. His hair had been dyed shoe-polish black, and he had dark circles under his eyes. He wore mismatched earrings and, judging by the splotches along his jawline, he also wore makeup. Very bad makeup. Even by New York subway standards he was weird.

Then he smiled and got even weirder. His teeth were an unforgettable blend of orange and yellow. Not one of them was straight. I suddenly realized I had seen them earlier that morning. He'd been standing on the platform and smiled at me when I got off the subway on my way to school.

Now it seemed like he had been waiting all day for me to come back. I know that sounds paranoid, but that's what it felt like.

I smiled politely as I stood up and headed for the escalator. I wasn't moving particularly fast because I didn't want to alert him and also because my backpack was loaded down with all the new textbooks that had been handed out on the first day of school.

Even though I was going away from him, I could hear his boots thud as he walked across the floor behind me. He was moving faster than I was, and the sound was getting closer.

I needed to slow him down, so I decided to use all those textbooks to my advantage. Just as I heard him about to reach me, I swung around with my backpack at the end of my outstretched arm to build as much force as possible. I was going to slam it right into the side of his head.

He didn't even flinch. He just reached out and stopped my bag with an open hand. For a skin-and-bones–looking guy, he was unbelievably strong. He ripped the backpack out of my hand and flung it across the floor.

Cool and calm, I told myself.

He made a move for me, and out of nowhere I flashed back to my Jeet Kune Do classes. I turned my body to the side, and when his fist went past me, I punched him right in the ribs. It must have been pretty hard because I actually heard ribs break.

I smiled because I knew this would knock him to the ground and let me run for help. Unfortunately, he didn't seem to know this. The broken ribs didn't bother him at all. He just stood there and flashed that crazy Crayola smile of his.

Cool and calm was no longer an option. It was time to be *freaked and frightened*!

He grabbed me by the shoulders and slammed me against the wall. I screamed for help, which got no response from him or anyone else. And just when I thought he couldn't be any creepier, he started to sniff the air around my face like he was some sort of wild animal.

"What do you want from me?" I wailed.

He tried to talk, but it was a struggle for him to form a word. Finally, he gurgled something that sounded like "Omaha." Then he yanked off my mom's necklace. The chain cut into the flesh along the back of my neck.

He started to say something else when a voice called out.

"Dude, you'll want to give that back. It's a family heirloom."

Creepy Joe and I both turned to see my rescuer. It was Natalie. Oddly enough, he seemed to recognize her. Because the second he saw her, he let go of me, smiled, and started sizing her up.

"I can tell by your genius expression that you know what I am," Natalie barked. I had no idea where this tough-girl attitude was coming from, but I was happy to see it on my side.

"What do you have to say for yourself?" she taunted. "Come on! Use your words!"

This frustrated him. He kept trying to say something, but the struggle was too hard. After a few tries, he gave up and just charged at her. He was fast. Right when he was about to slam into her, she twisted to the side and used his momentum to slam him into the tile wall.

"I'll call the police!" I yelled.

"Don't," Natalie said, looking right at me. "I've got this."

She turned back to face Creepy Joe, who was picking himself up off the ground. There was now a huge cut across his forehead. But for some reason there was no blood. He also had three fingers completely dislocated and pointing in different directions. This didn't seem to bother him either, as he calmly snapped each one back into place. When he was done he smiled again.

Natalie was completely unfazed.

"If you think you're some sort of tough guy Level 2 who can make his reputation by taking me out, you are sadly misinformed," she said. "You're an L3, and that's all you'll ever be. I don't know what you've heard, but there's no climbing back up the evolutionary ladder."

I had absolutely no idea what she was talking about. But he seemed to. And the taunting made him even angrier.

He ran straight at her again. This time she leveled him with an elbow across the face that sent him sprawling on the floor.

When she saw her sleeve, she was not happy.

"Look what your cheapo makeup did to my favorite shirt," she said as she pointed at a smear by her elbow. "I love this shirt. It's my first-day-of-school shirt. And that will not come out."

This time he was too woozy to get up. The blow to the head had really shaken him, and Natalie took advantage of this. She stepped over him and kneeled down so that her knees pinned his shoulders to the ground.

He snarled and spat and tried to break loose, but it was useless.

"Did he sniff you?" she asked.

At first the question didn't register.

"Did he sniff you?" she demanded more emphatically.

"Yeah," I said, creeped out by the memory. "Like a dog."

She looked down at him and shook her head.

"Get the vanilla," she told me, pointing at her bag on the floor. "It's in the front pocket."

"The vanilla extract from the morgue?" I asked, confused, as I dug around for it.

"It's more useful than you might imagine."

I found the bottle and then handed it to her. She jammed it up each of his nostrils and squirted until he sneezed and gagged.

"That should take care of that," she said. Next, she pulled one of his earrings tight, so that it stretched out his lobe. "Now, do I have your attention?"

He nodded.

"The way you roughed up my friend over there was not cool. I want to give you a little reminder so you don't make the same mistake again."

Without warning she yanked on the earring and in the process ripped off most of his ear. That's not an exaggeration. More than half his ear was now dangling from the earring in her hand.

"I want you to go back to where you belong and spread the word among all your little troll buddies that if any of you mess with me or my friends, some very bad things will happen. Very bad! Do you understand?"

He nodded slowly.

"Go ahead," she said. "Use your words."

He took a deep breath and, with a voice straight out of another world, slowly answered, "Un-der-stand."

"Good," she said as though everything was bright and cheery. "I'm glad we had this chance to talk. Now give me back her necklace."

She jerked the necklace from his hand and got off him. He scampered to his feet and ran away. In the final element of freaky, he didn't head for the exit. Instead, he ran into the subway tunnel toward Manhattan.

"Don't forget your ear," she called out to him. If he heard her, he was not coming back. Natalie tossed the ear into the darkness of the tunnel. Then she turned to me, and I did the only thing that seemed appropriate: I started to throw up onto the subway tracks.

"Go right ahead," she said. "It's really a lot to take in all at once. I threw up my first time too. Did he say anything to you?"

"Omaha," I said between retches.

She shook her head. "Not Omaha," she replied. "Omega."

"Why Omega?"

"It's actually a longer story than we have time for at the moment. But I promise I'll tell you everything. For right now, though, we need to get you aboveground quickly."

"Where are we going?" I asked.

"The tram."

"No way," I declared. "I am not riding in the dangling death cage."

"What?" she said with a smirk. "Are you really willing to take a chance that the next thing out of that tunnel is the F train, and not the creeper with a dozen of his friends? Because frankly, I don't think we're ready for that yet."

I looked into the darkness of the subway tunnel, and was terrified.

"Okay," I said softly. "Maybe the tram's not as bad as I think."

5

I'd Better Get Used to Creepy Guys Who Want to Kill Me

It turns out I was wrong about the Roosevelt Island tram. Riding it was *far more terrifying* than I had ever imagined. The floor rumbled, the cables creaked, and the entire car swayed from side to side in the wind. And just in case I forgot that I was dangling two hundred and fifty feet in the air, there were giant windows conveniently located on each side of the car to remind me. Luckily, I still had the subway attack fresh in my mind to keep me distracted.

"Just relax," Natalie whispered. "It's going to be all right." She was standing right next to me, trying to act normal while still being reassuring.

Whenever I went to ask her a question, she just waved me off. "We'll talk about it all when we get there."

"Can I at least ask where we're going?"

"Grayson's."

"Grayson from lunch?" I didn't quite see how a computer geek scared of white food was going to be of much help against an underground killing machine. "Why?"

"First of all, don't be like everybody else and underestimate him," she said. "Grayson is awesome. He's smart, funny, and talented. And he's off-the-charts loyal. Plus, he lives in Brooklyn, and we have got to get you out of Manhattan."

The next thirty minutes were a blur. I can only remember bits and pieces. I do know that somehow I survived the tram ride only to be told that we next had to take the subway to Brooklyn.

"We're going back underground? I thought you said that was bad."

"It will be safe," Natalie assured me. "Even if the creeper guessed we were coming here and ran full speed, it would take him at least another twenty minutes to reach this station. The tunnels don't intersect anywhere near here."

I guess it should have struck me as odd that Natalie knew so much about the layout of New York's subway tunnels. But I was too busy clinging to the "it will be safe" portion of her statement to notice.

Safe or not, she insisted we sit in the very front of the first car. And she turned so that she was in front of me and could see if anyone was coming toward us.

I was still in a fog when we made it to Grayson's. He lives in a brownstone in the Fort Greene section of Brooklyn.

"Come on in," he said when he opened the door. Then he shot Natalie a look. "You're only *three* days early."

"Sorry about that, but we kind of had to speed things up," Natalie said as we entered. "Are we alone?"

"Yes, but I don't know for how long," he answered, obviously frustrated. "I had arranged for everyone to be gone on Friday—"

She cut him off. "I know. This was supposed to happen in three days. Deal with it."

"How am I supposed to do that?" he asked, exasperated, nodding toward me. "I'm not ready for her to be here."

"You know, I'm in the room and can hear you," I reminded him.

"As I told you at lunch," Natalie said, "Grayson's a little lacking in the social skills."

"Oh, right, and you're so good. How about the social

skills in this text you sent?" He picked up his phone and read it aloud. "'Molly's orientation. Thirty minutes. Grayson's.' No explanation. No 'please.' No verbs."

"Listen, she was attacked in the subway station," Natalie said, cutting to the point. "He was a bad guy, and I don't think it's wise to leave her out there without some support and information. Besides, I kind of outrank you, so get over it."

"Attacked?"

"By a Level 3."

"You might have mentioned that in the text," he said, suddenly concerned. He turned to me with caring eyes that were surprisingly reassuring. "Are you okay?"

"I'm not sure," I answered honestly. "I don't really understand what's going on."

He gave me a quick look over, checking for any bumps or bruises. "What happened to your neck?" he asked.

I had forgotten about that. I reached up and ran my finger along the cut. The sting had dulled but still hurt. "He yanked off my necklace."

"We'd better clean it," he said. "Come on."

He led me into the kitchen. I leaned over the sink and held up the back of my hair while he ran some cool water over the wound.

"How do you know he's a Level 3?" he asked Natalie. "The teeth?"

"They were some kind of special," she said. "Quite the ad for daily flossing."

I stood up from the sink, and he handed me a paper towel. "Pat this gently along the wound. Don't rub, just pat."

"I know," I said with a smile. "My dad's a paramedic. He's kind of obsessive when it comes to first-aid training."

Grayson smiled. "First-aid training. That will come in handy."

Natalie nodded.

"Hey, I know what would come in handy," I said.

"What?"

"If you guys would stop talking about this like any of it makes sense and explain it to me instead."

"I'm sorry," Grayson said with a sigh. "It's just all so complicated. I don't know where to begin. That's why I've been working on my presentation for the last few weeks. So that we could explain all this in a way that would make sense to you."

"How can you have been working on it for weeks?" I asked. "We just met today."

He smiled and shared a look with Natalie. "Actually, we've been checking you out for nearly a year."

"Checking me out for what?" I asked.

"Why don't you just do the presentation," Natalie said, prodding.

"It's not—"

"I know," she said. "It's not perfect. But you're Grayson the Great. I'm sure it's still amazing. Way better than I could do with months to prepare."

"Okay," he said with a bashful smile, the flattery working like a charm. "But we'll have to watch in my room. It's still loaded on Zeus."

"Zeus?" I said.

"His computer. He named it." Then she whispered conspiratorially, "He acts like it's a person."

"I do not," he said as we walked down the hall toward his room.

"You gave it a birthday party," she said.

Grayson stopped walking for a moment. "Annual hard-drive maintenance and software upgrades do not count as a birthday party."

"No," she said. "But singing 'Happy Birthday' to it does."

He took a deep breath. They'd obviously been through this before. "You know I was testing the new voice-recognition software."

Natalie looked at me. "Birthday party."

I laughed for the first time since the attack.

"Pardon my messy room," Grayson said as he opened the door.

"Yeah, I know," I answered. "You weren't expecting me for three more days. I'm fine with a little mess."

Okay, "little mess" turned out to be something of an understatement. The room was a maze of books, maps, and electronics.

One wall was covered with a giant subway map. It wasn't like the color-coded ones on the walls in each station that show you which train to take. It was technical, with elevations and measurements. It also had stations marked that I didn't recognize. They were ones that had been closed down long ago.

The star of the room, though, was definitely Zeus, which took up an entire third of the floor space. It was an odd mix of high-tech and homemade. Different computers and custom parts had all been connected into one giant supercomputer, with three large high-def monitors.

"Tell him hello," Grayson whispered to me.

"Tell who?"

"Zeus."

"You want me to talk to your computer? Seriously?"

Natalie nodded for me to do it. So, even though I felt ridiculous, I went with it.

"Hello, Zeus."

"Hello, Molly," it answered in a human-sounding voice. "Welcome to Omega."

Again with the Omega, but more than a little cool that Zeus recognized my voice. My yearbook picture even popped up on-screen. Grayson was grinning proudly.

"How'd you pull that off?" Natalie asked.

"I recorded her voice today at lunch," he answered.

"Will somebody tell me what Omega is?" I demanded, trying to get them to focus on what was going on.

"That's what I'm about to explain," Grayson said. He pulled out a chair from his desk and offered it to me. He signaled Natalie to sit on the corner of his unmade bed.

Grayson picked up some index cards and stood by the computer like he was about to give a speech. Just before he started talking, he turned to check his appearance in a mirror on his dresser and fixed his hair with a comb he pulled from his back pocket.

"Good evening," he said, reading from the first card. (Apparently, Friday's session was scheduled for evening.) "For your safety and ours, what we're about to tell you must stay private. You can't tell anybody. First of all, no one would believe you. Second, it would put them in danger as well. Do you understand?"

I didn't, but I nodded anyway. "I think so."

Just then the door to the room flew open. I let out a frightened yelp that startled Grayson and sent his index cards flying.

"Did I miss it?"

I turned to see Alex. He was breathing heavily and had obviously been running.

"No," Natalie told him, "we're just getting started."

"I thought this was supposed to be on Friday," he said as he caught his breath.

"*Deal with it*, people," Natalie replied, her temper rising. "She got attacked by a Level 3."

Alex nodded and looked at me. "You okay?"

"I think so," I answered.

"Can we get on with this?" Grayson asked as he picked up his index cards. "My parents could come home at any minute with Wyatt and Van."

Natalie turned to me and shuddered as she said, "His brothers . . . pure evil."

"Sorry," Alex said. "I'll just clear off a spot over here."

He pushed an armful of junk off the edge of the bed

and sent it clattering across the hardwood floor. He took a seat and motioned for Grayson to resume.

"Where was I?" Grayson said as he tried to put the cards back in order. He checked his reflection in the mirror again and ran the comb back through his hair. Then he looked back at me.

"After much consideration, Natalie, Alex, and I would like to extend a formal invitation for you to join our Omega Team. The team's name comes from the final letter in the Greek alphabet because it's our responsibility to be the final word."

"The final word on what?" I asked.

Grayson shot a look at the other two and then back to me. "The final word on the undead."

I don't know how long I sat there with the big doofus expression on my face, but I'm sure it was for a while. Finally, I was able to ask, "You mean, like, zombies?"

"Actually, they hate being called that," he said. "But yes, that's what I mean."

I turned to Natalie and Alex. They both nodded. My first thought was that this was all a big practical joke. I didn't know why they would go to so much trouble to embarrass me, but that was the only thing that made sense.

"Since its founding," Grayson continued, "MIST has

been training select students to police and protect the undead citizens of New York City."

I'd had enough.

"Very funny," I said, with a combination of hurt and anger. "I get that I'm weird and people like to tease me. And maybe I was too eager to have new friends to notice that you were making fun of me. But you really shouldn't have gone to the trouble."

I started to get up, but Alex put a hand on my shoulder to stop me. "This isn't a joke," he said. "We know how hard this is to believe. Each one of us has been where you are right now. And each one of us had the same reaction. But trust us when we say it's true."

"That there are zombies living all over New York?"

"Not all over," Grayson said. "Only in Manhattan. And mostly underground or in the bottom floors of buildings. But that's getting a little ahead of ourselves."

"And just how many of these zombies are there?" I asked mockingly.

"One thousand one hundred and thirty-two," he answered. "According to the last census. But I think there are a lot more than that."

"The census?"

"Not the government one," Grayson said. "The 'Census

of the Undead' is taken by the Omegas every five years. It's one of our responsibilities. The problem is that most of them don't want to be counted."

"You guys really expect me to believe all this? You must think I'm the dumbest Lowbie of them all."

"Actually," Alex said, "we think you may be the smartest. That's why we want you on our team."

"Think about the guy in the subway today," Natalie said. "Nothing made him bleed. Nothing hurt him. Not even broken ribs or fingers twisted in every direction. It's because he isn't really alive. He's a zombie."

"If you join our team," Alex said, "we'll train you and teach you. The four of us will work together."

"To police and protect the undead?"

"That's right," Grayson answered. "There are three levels among the undead. Level 1s look and act just like us. For the most part, they want to live normal lives. That's where the *protect* comes in. We make sure they're able to do that."

"Level 2s look and act like us too," Alex said. "But they have no soul, which means they have no sense of right and wrong. That's where the *policing* comes in. Sometimes they can get out of hand and need to be stopped."

"And the Level 3s?" I asked. "Is that what you called the one who attacked me?"

"They're degraded 1s and 2s barely clinging to whatever bit of life they have," said Natalie. "They're more like the zombies you see in movies. A lot of them don't even realize they're undead. They can't pass for human too well, so they stay mostly underground and avoid coming out in the light of day."

"The presentation I have will take you through the whole history and explain what we know about them," Grayson said. "But we can only show it to you if you take a leap of faith. If you decide to join us."

"If you decide against it, we understand," Natalie said. "You can go back to your regular life, and we'll act like none of this ever happened."

I thought about this for a minute or so without saying a word. They stayed silent too and just sat there and watched me think it over.

"If this is true," I said, "which I don't believe, I don't really have a choice, anyway. I was already attacked for being an Omega even though I'm not one."

"It was a mistake," Natalie said. "Level 3s aren't too smart, and since I covered your scent with the vanilla, it won't happen again."

"Why would he even think I was one in the first place?" I asked.

Natalie held up my necklace. "Because you wore this."

"My mother's horseshoe necklace?" I asked, unable to make a connection.

"It's not a horseshoe," she said. She turned it upside down and I recognized the symbol instantly.

"It's an omega!" I said, realizing.

Natalie nodded.

"But why would my mom have . . ."

That was the exact moment when I started to believe.

"She was one, wasn't she? My mom was an Omega!"

"I can't tell you that," Natalie answered.

"Because you don't know? Or because you won't tell me?"

Natalie shook her head. "Because the identity of any Omega past or present cannot be revealed to anyone outside the group. That's for everybody's safety."

"Then you can tell me," I answered instantly. "And, Grayson, you can start your presentation. I'm in!"

Things You Should Never Touch in a Subway Tunnel and Other Lessons

When I told them I wanted to join, they exchanged happy looks and smiled. But before anyone could respond, we heard Grayson's parents come in the front door.

And they weren't alone.

To say that Grayson's little brothers are loud is like saying jet engines are kind of noisy. They sounded like a troop of howler monkeys as they raced down the hallway toward his room. Natalie told Alex to block the door to let me have a chance to reconsider.

"Are you sure?" she asked as the brothers started

slamming their bodies against the door to force their way in. "It's a big decision."

There wasn't much time to think about it. But I didn't really need any. I had never been more certain of anything in my life.

"Positive!"

Just then Alex lost the battle, the door flew open, and the brothers tumbled into the room. They were much smaller than their volume and strength had suggested. Both had big curly hair, thick glasses, and matching elementary school uniforms. They were arguing about whether or not dinosaurs were warm- or cold-blooded and wanted their big brother to settle the dispute.

"Stop!" Grayson quieted the pair as he pointed an angry finger at them. "How many times do I have to tell you about this?"

It was the same angry tone my sister uses whenever I interrupt her and her friends. Except, Grayson being Grayson, the interruption wasn't the part that he was angry about.

"Cold-blooded and warm-blooded are inaccurate terms," he continued. "It's 'endothermic' and 'ectothermic.' Got it? You're not in second grade anymore." (Okay, this was so unlike any argument I had ever had with Beth.)

The scolding quieted them for a few seconds until they

started another argument about who was to blame for using the wrong terms.

Eventually they left the room long enough for me to see Grayson's presentation. Even in its incomplete state, it was as impressive as Natalie had promised.

It was a full multimedia production, complete with pictures, graphics, and video. Some of it even had music and fancy editing. It explained the three levels of zombies and the history of the Omegas.

It was almost done when Grayson's brothers came back to argue about something else, and we decided to move out onto the stoop for some privacy.

I sat down on the top step and asked the one thing I was dying to know. "So tell me, was my mom an Omega?"

Natalie shook her head. "No, she was not *an* Omega." Then she flashed a huge grin. "She was *the* Omega."

"Seriously?"

"Absolutely," Grayson said. "She's a total legend."

"Depending on whether you were one of the living or one of the undead, she was either the most revered or most feared Omega ever," Alex added.

"Feared?" I could hardly believe it. "We're talking about my mom, right? The woman who made snickerdoodles for my birthday?"

"I haven't heard anything about her baking skills," Natalie answered, "but I have heard that she was the ultimate Zeke."

"Zeke?"

"It's from 'ZK,'" Alex explained. "Abbreviation for 'zombie killer.'"

I let this sink in for a moment and couldn't resist smiling. My mom was quite the mix: room mother, soccer coach, medical examiner, zombie killer. No wonder I turned out the way I did.

And now I was following in her footsteps.

Over the next six weeks, Omega training dominated my world. And while my complete lack of a social life left me with plenty of free time, training ate up enough of it that it affected my studies. This led to an oh-so-fun lecture from my dad about my midterm grades.

I blamed it on watching too much television and promised to fix them before my next report card. I don't normally lie to my dad, but I couldn't possibly tell him the truth. It's not like MIST wasn't already superdifficult. It turns out it's even harder when you have to squeeze all of your homework and studying in between training sessions with names like "Seven Ways to Kill a Zombie," "How to Remove Dead Flesh from Open Wounds," and my all-time fave: "Things You Should Never Touch in a Subway Tunnel." (Spoiler alert: "Pretty much everything.")

My new teammates took turns, so I worked with each one on different days.

Mondays and Fridays, I learned history and procedures from Grayson. To avoid interruptions from his brothers, we usually took long walks around Brooklyn while we talked. He explained that the Omegas were more like spies than police and that there was an unknown number of other teams. The only person who knew all the identities was the Prime Omega. The identity of the Prime Omega was top secret, and we had to communicate with him through special encryption software on Grayson's computer.

One Friday, Grayson told me the story of how the zombies originated. We were walking through the Prospect Park Zoo and had just stopped in front of the sea lions.

"It all began in 1896," he started to explain. "A group of miners was digging one of New York's first subway tunnels when an explosion killed all thirteen men in the crew."

He stopped midstory when a family came up and stood next to us at the railing.

"Let Daddy take your picture in front of the seals," said the father.

Grayson turned to him, and, knowing what I knew

about his lack of social grace, I fully expected him to correct the father by pointing out that they were, in fact, sea lions and not seals. I was pleasantly surprised when instead he offered to take their picture so that the whole family could be in it.

"Everyone smile," he said, before adding, "including you *sea lions*." (All right, so he couldn't totally resist. After all, this is Grayson we're talking about.)

He took the picture and handed the camera back to the father. A few moments later, they were walking toward the next exhibit, and I said to Grayson, "I knew you were going to correct him."

Grayson just smiled and resumed the story of the subway miners. "Anyway, the explosion that killed them also blasted open a deep pocket of Manhattan schist."

"What's Manhattan schist?" I asked.

"It's an extremely dense and strong type of bedrock," he answered. "The only place on earth it's found is underneath Manhattan. Without it, New York couldn't have all of its skyscrapers. It's what makes the city possible. And it's also what makes the undead possible."

"What do you mean?"

"Some energy force from the minerals in that bedrock brought the miners back to life," he explained. "But they weren't really alive. They were *undead*."

"And Manhattan schist is still what keeps them from dying?" I asked.

He nodded. "That's why the undead can't leave. And why they stay mostly at ground level or below. That rock is like their oxygen. The farther away from it they are, the weaker they get."

We looked out at the sea lions for a minute, and I pointed out something that I had observed.

"You never call them zombies, do you?"

He shook his head and smiled, maybe a little pleased I had noticed. "No, I don't."

"Why not?"

"Because they don't like it," he said simply. "At least the ones I've talked to. When you hear the word 'zombie,' you think of bad horror movies and flesh-eating monsters. That's just not accurate. I figure if they don't like it, the least I can do is respect that."

"Just like sea lions don't like to be called seals," I pointed out.

"That's exactly right." He turned to a sea lion and called down to it, "You hate that, don't you?"

The sea lion barked back, almost as if he was answering, and we both laughed.

Unlike Grayson, Alex had no problem using the

z-word. That was pretty obvious when I showed up for my first lesson: "Seven Ways to Kill a Zombie."

Don't get me wrong. Alex is a total sweetheart and an incredibly nice person. I just think four years of hand-to-hand combat with the undead have made him not too worried about hurting their feelings.

Alex was in charge of my physical training. We did martial arts together on Tuesdays, and for Thursdays he convinced me to join the school's fencing team. He said it would be good to get weapons practice. I thought I'd hate it, but it's awesome.

"Zombies feel no pain, and most of their organs are no longer functioning," he told me that first day. "So most traditional methods of fighting are useless. When it comes to killing zombies, it's all about going for the head."

We were lined up on the mat in traditional combat positions.

"I'm going to come at you like a zombie," he said. "I want you to show me what you can do."

I looked up at him. Very up. He was at least six inches taller and a hundred pounds heavier.

"It's not exactly a fair fight," I offered.

"It never is," he answered with a confident smile. Of

course he was confident; he didn't know that I had been a star pupil in my Jeet Kune Do class.

The last thing he said as he moved toward me was "Remember to go for the head."

The philosophy of Jeet Kune Do revolves around fluid motion. You are taught to imagine yourself to be like water, which is exactly what I did as he approached me. I dipped down low, spun to the left, and popped up right next to him. This caught him completely off guard. Before he could react, I landed two punches on his jaw and sent him sprawling across the mat.

"You mean like that?" I said, more than a little pleased with myself.

It took him a moment to answer, but when he did he was smiling. He was rubbing the side of his face, but he was smiling.

"Yeah," he said. "Like that."

Wednesdays and Saturdays I did field practice with Natalie. She was great. She taught me how to identify the undead, how to follow someone without being seen, and how to find "indicators." Indicators are beyond cool and are what you use to find former Omegas.

Once you're an Omega, you're one for life. The saying is "Omega today, Omega forever." When you graduate from MIST, you become what's known as a "sleeper." Sleepers are available to help current Omegas. But since everyone's identity must be kept secret, you have to use a code to find the sleepers. The key element of that code is an indicator.

I saw my first indicator one Saturday morning when Natalie pointed out a small red Omega symbol that had been spray painted on the sidewalk.

"Here's one," she said.

"That's an indicator?" I asked. If you didn't know what you were looking for, you'd think it was just a stray mark left over by a work crew.

"No, that's called a 'standpoint,'" she said. "But if you stand on that spot, you should be able to see the indicator."

"Isn't that kind of dangerous?" I asked. "The symbol being so public?"

"The key to indicators is that they're hidden in plain sight. If they weren't, we wouldn't be able to find them. Besides, I think you'll see that it's not as easy as it sounds."

We'll call that an understatement.

I stood on the symbol for about five minutes, looking in every direction, searching for anything that might be an indicator, but nothing looked like a code or a clue to me.

"Okay," I finally admitted. "I give up."

Natalie smiled. "What about that shop right over there?" she asked as she pointed at a plant and flower store called Home Gardens.

"What about it?"

"Take the last three letters of 'home' and the first two of 'gardens' and what do you get?"

"O-m-e-g-a. Oh my God, it spells 'Omega'!" I couldn't believe it. Suddenly it seemed so incredibly obvious, like when you find out how a magic trick is done and can't believe that it fooled you.

"You got it," she said. "The woman who runs the shop was an Omega about ten years ago. She comes into the school sometimes to lecture to the botany class."

"Do we go inside and introduce ourselves?" I asked.

"No! The rule is that you only make contact with a sleeper if there is an imminent need," Natalie explained. "That's crucial. We have to protect our identities and theirs. For now, you just lock it away in your memory until you need it someday."

The concept of hidden in plain sight is important. In fact, the key to virtually every Omega code hangs right out in the open in most of the classrooms at MIST. It's the periodic table of elements.

"You're going to have to learn the periodic table," Grayson told me one day. His parents and brothers were at soccer practice, so we were kicking back and drinking cream sodas in his kitchen.

I cracked a smile. "That's easy. I already know the periodic table. It has one hundred eighteen different elements, and each one of those has an atomic number, symbol, and weight."

"I know you know what it is," he answered. "But I mean you're *really* going to have to know it. Memorize it inside and out."

"That's easy," I said with a laugh as I repeated myself. "I already know the periodic table. If you want to test me, feel free."

He gave me a skeptical look. "Okay. I'm going to list off a series of atomic numbers. I want you to tell me which elements they represent."

It was obvious he thought I couldn't do it, so I just played along and said, "I'll try my best."

Without taking a breath he rattled off, "Four, seventy-four, eighteen, seventy-five."

Just as quickly I answered, "Beryllium, tungsten, argon, and rhenium."

His jaw fell open a bit. He was impressed, but he wasn't

going to quit so easily. "That's good . . . but can you write out their symbols?"

I picked up a pencil and quickly wrote the symbols: "Be" for beryllium, "W" for tungsten, "Ar" for argon, and "Re" for rhenium. When I looked down, I was surprised to see that except for one extra *R*, they spelled out a word: BeWArRe. "Beware!" I said, a bit louder than I had intended.

"Very nice," he said. "To the Omegas the numbers four, seventy-four, eighteen, seventy-five are code for 'Beware.'"

I thought it was a pretty cool little code.

"Can you do it in reverse?" he asked. "What code would you use to say 'Help'?"

"I'd go helium, lithium, and phosphorus. That's two, three, fifteen."

He shook his head. "How did you know that so quickly?" he asked. "You haven't taken chemistry yet."

"My mom," I answered. "She made me memorize the periodic table the summer she was in the hospital. She drilled me on it over and over again. I had to know all the parts, but I got fifty cents for every one I got right. The periodic table earned me fifty-nine dollars."

Grayson thought about this for a moment and smiled. "That explains it."

"What explains what?" I asked.

"Your mom," he answered. "She was training you."

"What do you mean?"

"For this," he said as if it couldn't be more obvious. "She was giving you a head start on your Omega training."

I wondered if that could possibly be true. Did my mother suspect I would end up here? If she did, some of her decisions suddenly made more sense. The Jeet Kune Do classes came in handy when Alex and I were training.

And when we were in the field, Natalie said I had to know my way around every inch of Manhattan. I had to know which subways ran to which stations and where all the little parks were located, because they were favorite meeting spots of the undead.

Brownies and Girl Scouts may not know the parks, but Junior Birders do. My time with the Audubon Society had taken me to every little park and green space on the island.

I realized that Grayson was right. My mother had been preparing me for this my whole life. Maybe, just maybe, I could go from geek to Zeke.

The last day of my training was a Saturday. Natalie and I were walking in midtown, not far from the morgue, when I found a standpoint on the sidewalk. Someone had used a stick to draw an Omega symbol into the sidewalk when the cement was still wet.

"Standpoint," I said.

Natalie looked down and smiled. "I've never seen this one before."

After a second, we both said it at the same time: "Race you!"

We stood on the standpoint and scanned the neighborhood for the indicator. It only took about forty-five seconds until I said, "Got it."

I gave Natalie a couple of minutes, but she couldn't find it.

"I don't see it," she said, her pride a little wounded.

"That's because you didn't spend five years in Catholic school," I explained.

I pointed out a bakery across the street. In the corner of the window was an old New York license plate.

"Kind of a strange place for a license plate," I said.

"I guess," she replied. "Maybe it was from their first delivery truck."

"R-E-V-2-2-1-3," I said, reading the plate aloud.

"What about it?"

"It's a verse from the Bible. 'REV' is the book of Revelation, then chapter twenty-two, verse thirteen. 'I am the Alpha and the Omega.' Check out the name of the bakery."

Natalie looked at the sign above the door. "Alpha Bakery. Very nice."

"Thank you," I said, trying to convey modesty but failing miserably.

"Do you know what that means?" she asked.

"That my teacher has done a great job showing me how to spot an indicator?"

"Well, yes. But it also means something much more important."

I looked at her expectantly. "What?"

"It means you're ready for your final exam."

Ω 7

Killing Time

I don't mean to brag, but as far as training goes, I pretty much killed it. Grayson told me it normally takes six to eight weeks to finish, and I was done in four. Of course, most Omega trainees haven't been secretly prepared for it by their zombie-hunter mothers, so I tried not to let it go to my head. Still, it was kind of cool. And if you haven't noticed, "cool" and "my life" aren't very well acquainted.

The biggest advantage to finishing early was that the team wasn't ready for my final exam. That meant, with the exception of Thursday's fencing practice, I had a week completely free to catch up on schoolwork. And, yes, I do realize being excited about having time to catch up on schoolwork might explain why "cool" and "my life" are such strangers.

Of course, having time to catch up and actually taking advantage of it are two totally different things. It seemed that no matter how hard I tried to focus, I could not stop thinking about my mom, the Omegas, and what my life as a zombie killer might be like. Then, after fencing practice, I did something really stupid.

I went back to the Alpha Bakery.

I know that Natalie told me there should be no contact unless there was an *imminent need*, but I *needed* to do something Omega based or I thought I would burst. Besides, I wasn't actually planning on making contact. I had an excuse. It was my father's birthday, and although there are about a hundred bakeries closer to our apartment, I needed a cake.

Before I went in, I stopped at the standpoint to make sure I hadn't misread the clue. I hadn't. The only thing that could possibly refer to Omega was the license plate with the coded Bible verse. My plan was to go into the bakery, get a cake, and get out. Since the baker would never know I was an Omega, there would be no hint I had broken any rules and I would still have the thrill of making a secret connection.

I walked in, and a bell over the door announced my arrival. The smell was delicious. A man looked up from a sheet of fresh-baked cookies.

"Can I help you?" he asked.

I was determined to play it cool. "I'm looking for a birthday cake . . . for my pops." (Apparently, something in my head suggested "pops" would sound cool. It didn't.)

"We have a book over here with different cakes you can order," he said. "How soon is his birthday?"

"Today," I said sheepishly.

"All right," he offered with a smile. "Let's skip the book and see what we've already got made."

There was a display case with about eight cakes in different sizes. They all looked amazing, and I started to worry about the price. Then he gave me something much bigger to worry about.

"So, you go to MIST."

I panicked. My *brilliant* plan relied on him not knowing I was an Omega. But somehow he had spotted me. Then I realized my mistake. He must have seen me go to the standpoint and make the ID. When I came in, he thought it was a signal that I was in trouble.

"I'm sorry," I stammered. "I don't really need . . . I mean, I do need a cake, but there aren't any . . . you know . . . zombies.

I mean, *undead*. It's just, I figured out the code about Revelation, and, you know Natalie, my trainer, missed it, and I'm waiting for my test and I thought . . ."

This was when I noticed the look of absolute confusion on the man's face. Something was terribly wrong. So I just stopped talking, as if I had reached the end of a sentence or had at least completed a coherent thought.

He waited for a moment before asking, "What are you talking about?"

I very cleverly responded with, "What are *you* talking about?"

"I thought we were talking about a birthday cake."

I put my hands on my hips. "Then what made you ask if I went to MIST?"

He gave me a "duh" look and pointed at my shirt. That would be the shirt that read MIST FENCING. (The shirt is actually kind of cute. On the back it says, FENCERS ARE SHARP, but that's really not important to this part of the story.)

"Oh," I responded as I quickly tried to think of a way out of the situation. We've already established that thinking fast on my feet isn't exactly a strength. Luckily, a rescuer came from the back room.

"Tommy," he said, putting a hand on the shoulder of

the guy with the perplexed look still on his face, "can you help unload the boxes from the delivery truck? I'll take care of this customer."

He turned to me and continued his save. "You're looking for a birthday cake, right? With a zombie theme?"

"Right," I answered, relieved. "My pops is really into zombies." (Again with the "pops." Argghhh.)

"Sure thing," Tommy said as he disappeared into the back, no doubt thrilled to be away from the psycho.

Once he was gone, the man behind the counter looked down at me and actually glowered.

"You're only supposed to make contact when you have an imminent need," he reminded me. "Do you have one?"

"I really do need a birthday cake," I said before adding, "imminently."

He leaned forward with an even angrier look. "Let me rephrase that: Do you have a need worth the risk of possibly exposing the identities of two Omegas?"

I shook my head. Then I began to worry that this might lead to actual trouble. During one of his procedures lessons, Grayson described a whole suspension process with review boards. I wasn't even a full member yet, and I might have already blown my chance.

"Please don't tell anyone. I promise I won't do it again."

I gave him my best pleading eyes, which seemed to do the trick. There was something in the way he looked at me. A recognition.

He stared for a moment, lost in a thought as a smile slowly grew across his face. Then he put a name to that memory: "Rosemary Collins."

Now it was my turn to smile.

"My mother," I said, confirming what he already knew. "We have the same mismatched eyes."

"No," he replied, shaking his head. "You have the same everything. It's like I'm back in the eighth grade."

I knew I had my mother's eyes, but to hear that we shared other features was nice. Also nice was the fact that it seemed to have changed his mood for the better.

"You knew my mom in eighth grade?"

"That's when she asked me to be on her Omega Team," he answered, a large part of his attention still pleasantly reliving the memory.

"Did you think it was a practical joke when she asked?" I wondered. "I did when they asked me."

"Absolutely," he said with a booming laugh. Then he stopped and looked more serious. "But it isn't a joke. It's important. And so is following the procedures and protocols."

"I know," I answered. "I really am sorry. Please don't tell."

"You should know better," he replied, although less harshly than before. "How long have you been an Omega?"

"I just finished my training," I answered. And then, realizing I might not be able to brag about it to anybody else, I added, "It took me four weeks."

He did a double take, and smiled. "You completed all of your training in four weeks? You've got more in common with your mom than your looks."

This actually made me blush.

"Now, is it really your dad's birthday?" he asked.

I nodded. "Yes, sir."

"Let's get him a cake."

We picked out a red velvet cake with cream cheese frosting—Dad's favorite. The baker gave me a huge discount and reminded me I should not come back unless the situation truly demanded it.

As I headed out the door, I turned back and asked him a question. "Out of curiosity, what made you become a baker?"

He smiled. "What do you think?"

"Does it have something to do with the lecture on the first day of school? When everybody eats the bread?"

He nodded. "It has everything to do with it." Then he winked at me, and I hurried home.

Beth was not pleased that I was forty minutes late, but her mood brightened considerably when she saw the killer cake.

She was hard at work at the stove and waved a wooden spoon toward a cutting board on the counter. "Start chopping mushrooms."

We were making beef Stroganoff, which is kind of an inside joke in our family. My mom had many talents, but cooking was not one of them. Baking she could do, but actual meals, not so much. Dad has always run the kitchen, which is great because part of his job as a paramedic is taking turns cooking for the other guys in the station house. He's an awesome cook.

One year he even won a contest for the entire New York City Fire Department and was asked to do a cooking demonstration on a local morning TV show. Beth and I got to skip school and go to the studio. It was a big thrill. As he was cooking, the host of the show asked him if there was anything he couldn't make, and Dad joked that he knew how to make everything but beef Stroganoff.

Mom latched on to this in the way that only she could. She decided that she would master beef Stroganoff and make it her one specialty. She researched online, consulted friends, and even took a class at a cooking school, just to learn that one recipe so she could surprise my dad on his birthday. Of course, it never occurred to her that the reason Dad didn't make beef Stroganoff was because he didn't like it. And, of course, it never occurred to Dad to tell Mom. So every year, on his birthday, she pretended to be a gourmet chef and he pretended to like beef Stroganoff.

We've offered to make him something he actually likes, but he insists, so that's what we make.

He also insists that for his birthday, there are no friends or relatives, no Internet or phone calls—just the three of us and the Stroganoff.

The deluxe cake, though, was a welcome addition. Before he blew out the candles, he closed his eyes to make a wish. Then he turned to the living room to see if it had come true.

"Drat," he said. (Only Dad still uses a term like "drat.")

"What did you wish for?" I asked.

"Mrs. Papadakis and the Leather Bags . . . in their bathing suits."

Even my sister laughed at that one.

We had a great evening, talking, laughing, and just being goofy. And because of his no-phones-or-Internet rule, I didn't get the message from Natalie until the next morning.

In typical Natalie fashion, the message wasn't chatty. There was just an address, a time, and two words in all capital letters: FINAL EXAM.

Ω8

If You've Ever Wanted to Know a Good Place to Meet Zombies ...

Just as I'd suspected, Natalie's building had a doorman. His maroon jacket and cap had gold braid that matched the stripe down each side of his pants. His name tag said "Hector" and his smile said that he had no idea he was giving me such bad news.

"What was that?" I asked with a gulp, hoping that I'd misheard him.

"They're waiting for you in apartment 12-B," he repeated. "You can take the elevator to your left." Unfortunately, that's exactly what I'd heard the first time too.

"Thanks," I mumbled as I began my walk of doom toward the elevator.

I hadn't even thought to ask Natalie what floor she lived on. The message had her address and said to be there Saturday at four o'clock. I'd assumed we were going to meet in the lobby and go somewhere for my final exam. Now Hector was telling me the meeting was a full nine floors above my normal limit.

My knees got weak just thinking about it.

Confession time: While I wasn't lying when I said I'd killed it during training, I may have glossed over the fact that my fear of heights had been a major problem. That's because sometimes the only way to escape the undead is to go up into buildings high enough that the Manhattan schist no longer gives them power. That usually means about ten to fifteen floors. My instinct to do everything but go up was something I'd have to conquer. I knew this.

I just didn't know I'd have to conquer it so soon.

But I realized that as much as I dreaded it, there was no way I could possibly pass my final exam without actually going to Natalie's apartment to take it. So I got on the elevator, pressed the button for twelve, and held my breath.

I eventually made it to 12-B. Alex opened the door,

greeting me with a big smile. "Come on in," he said. Then he called out to an unseen room, "She passed the first part!"

"What was the first part?" I asked.

"We weren't sure you'd make it up this high."

"I'm still not sure," I answered, only half joking. "Either you're wearing makeup or it's actually affecting my vision."

"No, your vision's fine," he said with a laugh. "I *am* wearing makeup. It's part of the test," he added cryptically.

Before I could begin to figure out what that meant, he led me through an apartment that was so amazing, I almost forgot my fears. There was a music room with a grand piano and cello, and a library with overstuffed chairs and floor-to-ceiling bookcases. The living room even had a wall of windows with a balcony that over-looked Central Park.

"Crazy, isn't it?" he said, shaking his head and pointing at the balcony. "It's like something out of a movie."

"Yeah," I answered as I stepped back to avoid the dizzying view. "A *horror* movie."

We reached a large bathroom with side-by-side sinks. Natalie was leaning over one to check the mirror as she carefully applied eye shadow. Grayson was at the other, rinsing his mouth with some orange liquid. The fact that all four of us fit comfortably in the bathroom is a pretty good sign it was nothing like our place in Queens.

"Look who made it," Alex announced as we walked in.

"I told you," Grayson half spoke and half gargled.

"Perfect timing," Natalie said as she turned to us. "How does my makeup look? Be honest."

I hoped this wasn't part of the test, because she looked terrible. My experience with makeup was absolutely zero, but even I could tell this was bad. Luckily, Alex answered first.

"Awful," he said. "You look like a corpse."

I expected Natalie to slug him, but instead she smiled and asked, "You're not just saying that, are you?"

Grayson spit the mouthwash into the sink and then patted a washcloth across his lips. "Nope. You look totally dead."

"But still cute," she added.

"Oh yeah," Alex answered, rolling his eyes. "Dead . . . but cute."

"What about me?" Grayson flashed a big smile, revealing that the liquid had turned his teeth the same blend of yellow and orange as the teeth of the zombie who had attacked me in the subway station. "Do I look cute too?"

"No. You look hideous."

"Nice," he replied. "Hideous is exactly what I was going for."

I couldn't have been more confused. "Let me get this straight," I said, trying to hide my nervousness by sounding carefree and humorous. "For my final exam we're doing really bad makeovers?"

Natalie gave me a finger wag. "You wish it were that easy. No, for your final exam, we're going to a party. The makeovers are so we can get in."

"What kind of party needs bad makeovers?"

"A *flatline* party," Alex said.

"I'm guessing that's not some kind of Sweet Sixteen."

"Flatline parties are for the undead," Grayson explained. "Their name comes from the flat line that appears on a heart monitor when a patient dies. These parties are their only opportunity to come together in a group and just be themselves."

"They like to say that the only thing with a beat is the music," Alex added. "Strictly zombies. No breathers allowed." ("Breather" is undead slang for the living.)

"Which is why we need to look dead," I answered, finally getting it. "So we can crash the party."

"Exactly," Natalie replied. "As part of your final exam, you have to pass yourself off as undead for thirty minutes."

"Great," I said halfheartedly. "Acting and makeup. My two favorite things."

Suddenly, I was worried. I'd thought my test was going to be about finding standpoints and breaking codes. Things I knew I could ace. I had absolutely no confidence I could convince a group of zombies that I was one of them. What if I failed? I wondered if any retakes were allowed.

The three of them took turns helping me with my makeup. They used foundation, powder, and eye shadow to give my face a hollow, bloodless appearance, and then rubbed some gel in my hair to make it look dried out and frizzy.

When they finished, they scanned me over to make sure they hadn't missed anything.

"How do I look?" I asked.

Grayson smiled and then answered, "To *die* for."

The others groaned as they turned to him.

"You've been waiting all day to use that joke, haven't you?" Natalie asked.

"It's funny," he said. "Why should it matter when I thought of it?"

"Because it matters," Alex said.

While they continued to give him a hard time, I stood

up and looked at myself in the mirror. Surprisingly, I did look kind of dead. Maybe I could pull this off after all. "So, where is this party?"

"Good question," Alex answered. "As part of the whole no-breathers policy, they keep that information pretty secret."

"But we can find out," Grayson added. "That is, *if* you know how to get to J. Hood Wright Park."

He said it like a challenge, and I couldn't help but laugh. Alex and Grayson had been trying to stump me ever since Natalie bragged that I knew the city parks better than they did.

"Is this part of the test?"

"Why?" asked Alex. "Don't you know the answer?"

"Yeah," Grayson said eagerly. "Don't you?"

I paused for a second to get their hopes up and then said, "Actually, it depends on whether you want to enter by the rec center on Fort Washington Avenue or near the overlook on Haven Avenue," dashing their hopes. "Personally, I'd recommend the rec center. To get there we can get on the C train at 72nd Street. Switch over to the A at 168th. Continue north toward Washington Heights and get off at 175th."

Natalie cackled. "You only make yourself look silly

when you try to stump her," she said as she gave me a fist bump. "I told you she was a natural."

A natural, I thought. My confidence was growing.

We got to the park at that time of day when the city is its most beautiful. It was just before sunset and the sky had an orange glow that made the George Washington Bridge look like a painting at the Met. I was able to admire it for all of about thirteen seconds before Natalie took charge.

"The test starts now," she said. "Find the zombies."

A lump formed in the back of my throat. This was really happening.

I tried to come up with a strategy. The park stretches for three blocks on each side. Because a cluster of buildings in the middle blocks your view, you can see only about a third of it at a time. I decided to start in one corner and walk toward the center.

"Don't make it obvious that you're looking," Alex said. "Act natural."

Yeah, I thought. *Nothing's more natural than hunting zombies in a park full of children.*

On the playground, kids were chasing one another back and forth across a mini-size version of the George Washington Bridge. Their laughter filled the air, and I felt the urge to protect those children. I scanned the parents watching them play, but didn't see anyone who looked out of the ordinary.

We walked through an archway to the other side of the buildings and came to a table where three white-haired men were playing an intense game of dominoes. One was singing along with a Spanish song that played on the radio. They may have been old, but they were very much among the living.

Trying to act "natural," I pretended to watch the domino game. Meanwhile, I was able to scan another third of the park. A group of kids was playing baseball, a family was cleaning up after a birthday party, and a couple was pushing a stroller along the walkway. Once again, all were living.

I was stumped.

I turned to the others, who were also pretending to watch the domino game.

"Are you certain?" I asked them quietly.

Natalie nodded.

Then I remembered something.

"Schist," I said.

All three of them smiled.

In the corner of J. Hood Wright Park is a large outcropping of Manhattan schist. In fact, it's one of the largest aboveground formations anywhere. I looked toward the rocks and then toward Natalie. She nodded again.

The domino game ended, and I gave a little polite applause for the winner. Then I started to walk to the southwest corner of the park.

The rocks were the color of pencil lead, and had been smoothed by centuries of wind and rain. Two little kids were climbing on one corner of them, and on the opposite side were two couples.

At first glance you wouldn't think there was anything unusual about the couples, but I remembered my field training with Natalie. The first thing I noticed was that despite warm weather, all of them were wearing long sleeves. The undead often do this to protect their skin. Then I saw that one of the guys was wearing makeup and had done a bad job blending it in along the neckline. Finally, when one of the girls laughed, I saw that her teeth looked just like Grayson's.

I sat down on a bench across from them, and the others joined me. We acted normal, like a group of friends having a relaxing Saturday.

"Nice work," Grayson whispered.

"Are they going to have the party here?" I asked.

Alex shook his head. "No. This is just where they meet

before they go. We're going to have to follow them to the party."

And just when I thought the test couldn't get harder, he added, "We'll have to go down into Dead City."

The City That Really Never Sleeps

We're going into Dead City?" I asked nervously. "Really?"

Alex gave me an encouraging pat on the back. "Don't worry. It's not as bad as it sounds."

"Good," I replied. "Because it sounds creepy, gross, and disgusting."

"Oh," Natalie chimed in, "then it *is* as bad as it sounds."

"Yeah," added Grayson. "Creepy, gross, and disgusting pretty much nails it."

The three of them laughed.

"I'm glad my final exam amuses you all," I said as I joined them and laughed too.

Dead City, or DC, is what the Omegas call the maze of abandoned tunnels, sewers, aqueducts, and catacombs that wind their way underneath Manhattan. It's where zombies are free to move around without attracting attention from the living and where the bedrock walls of schist to recharge their bodies.

Dead City is also incredibly dangerous.

Omegas are allowed to go there only in groups of three or more. Natalie, Grayson, and Alex talked about it during training, but this was going to be my first actual visit. And if I'm totally honest, I'll admit that as creepy, gross, and disgusting as Dead City sounded, part of me was excited to see what it was like.

First, though, we had to keep an eye on the four zombies in the park. They were our key to finding the flatline party. For a group of undead, they were a pretty lively bunch. They were joking and laughing about something when a man approached them. He talked to them for a moment before he continued walking toward the middle of the park. The four of them, however, headed in the opposite direction, toward the street.

"Here's the next part of your test," Alex said. "He just told them where the party is. What do we do?"

The three of them looked at me.

"Follow," I said.

"Him or them?"

I hesitated for a second, worried that it might be a trick question. "Them."

"Okay," Alex said. "Show us what you've got."

I looked at Natalie, and she gave me a confident nod. I knew I had to take charge and show them the surveillance skills she had taught me.

"A-B shadow technique," I said, using the terminology from training. "Grayson and me in the first group, Natalie and Alex in the second."

From her smile I could tell that I was off to a good start.

Grayson and I waited on the bench for about thirty seconds before we began to follow the four zombies to the street. Thirty seconds after that, Natalie and Alex started following us. That's the key to A-B shadow technique. Because they were following us, Alex and Natalie were too far back to be seen by the people we were following. Every two blocks our two groups swapped places, making it less likely for them to notice any of us.

"You're doing great," Grayson said as we walked away from the park down Haven Avenue. "Really great."

"Thanks." I figured Grayson might offer moral support. That was partly why I picked him to be in my group.

We followed for about six blocks until the four of them turned down an alley. I kept an eye on what they were doing while Grayson bent over to tie his shoelace. This was the signal for Alex and Natalie to catch up to us.

One of the zombies lifted a grate from the ground, and the four of them quickly climbed down through the opening. The last one pulled the grate back over his head as he disappeared underneath. By the time Natalie and Alex reached us, the zombies were gone.

"Right over there," I told them. "All four went down through a grate in that alley."

"What do we do now?" Natalie asked.

"We've got to hurry up and go down there so we can follow them underground," I said.

"How do we do that and keep them from seeing us?" asked Alex.

This one stumped me for a moment before I figured it out. "It won't matter if they see us down there, because they'll assume we're undead, just like they are."

"Good answer," Alex said. "You're thinking like an Omega."

So far the test was going well, but I knew it was about to get a whole lot tougher once we got underground.

Alex pulled up the grate, which turned out to be much heavier than it looked. It opened up on a narrow shaft that went deep enough into the ground that I couldn't see the bottom. Iron rungs had been built into the side of the shaft and formed a ladder.

"I'll go first," Grayson offered.

"No," I said. "It's my test. I'm going first."

Alex pointed his flashlight down, but even with the light, I still couldn't tell how deep it was.

"Piece of cake," I said confidently, trying to convince myself as much as them.

I took a deep breath and started climbing down. One by one the others followed, with Alex going last. He was just pulling the grate back on at the top when I reached the bottom.

It took a minute or so for my eyes to adjust. Even when they did, everything was still mostly darkness and shadows. A few hundred yards away I could see a faint light bobbing up and down. It was a flashlight being carried by one of the zombies we had followed.

"This way," I said, pointing down the tunnel.

I started to walk, and my first step was right into a pool of water. Luckily, Natalie managed to grab my arm and kept me from falling in. As it was, my jeans were soaking wet all the way up above my left knee.

"Please tell me this isn't sewage," I said.

Alex laughed. "Believe me, you'd know if it was." He shined his flashlight across the ceiling. We were in a rounded tunnel about eight feet high in the middle. It must have been old, because instead of concrete it was made out of bricks. "It's just rainwater. I think we're in the Old Croton Aqueduct."

His light illuminated a narrow walkway on one edge of the tunnel. On the positive side, it was above the waterline, so it was mostly dry. On the negative, the curve of the wall made you walk with a severe tilt to the left. Within a few minutes my neck was starting to hurt.

As we walked, I tried to keep a mental map of where we were, but without buildings and streets to go by, it was impossible. Even though one of the world's busiest cities was only thirty feet above our heads, it felt like we were all alone on some alien planet.

Eventually the aqueduct met up with an abandoned subway tunnel, and we were finally able to stand up straight and stretch out. I rubbed my throbbing neck as I tried to figure out which way to go.

"Remember not to rub your neck at the party," said Grayson. "Zombies feel no pain, which means their muscles don't ache."

I would have completely forgotten that. Still, since it was just the four of us now, I kept massaging it. There was some lighting in this tunnel, which made it easier to see where we were going. Unfortunately, it also made it impossible to see the zombies' flashlight.

We were on our own. I wasn't sure about the grading scale for the exam, but I was pretty certain it'd be an F if I got everybody lost in Dead City.

"What next?" Alex said.

"First of all," I snapped, angrier than I intended, "I need you to be quiet and still."

Alex smiled, not at all offended by my attitude. He was happy that I was taking charge.

We all stopped moving and talking, and Dead City became even eerier. I closed my eyes, and one by one I tried to identify and eliminate the sounds I heard.

First was the steady flow of water along the aqueduct. If you forgot where you were, it sounded just like a waterfall up in the mountains. Next I could hear the faint echo of a subway train rushing along a distant tunnel. One by one I went through the sounds until I heard the one I was searching for.

"Got it," I said.

The others hadn't picked up on it yet. "Got what?" asked Natalie.

"The only thing with a beat." I pointed down the abandoned subway tunnel toward the faint thumping. "Music."

They listened for a moment and then smiled when they heard it too. We followed the sound, which gradually got louder as we got closer. Along the way, we met up with more zombies coming from different directions toward the party. I got nervous but tried to hide it. I also kept telling myself the same thing over and over.

Do not rub your neck!

When we finally reached the party, I was speechless. I'm not sure what I was expecting to find, but I know it was nothing like what we actually came across.

First of all, it was beautiful.

The party was being held in an abandoned subway station unlike any I had ever seen. The walls and archways were covered with gorgeous tiled mosaics, while the ceiling had brass chandeliers and stained-glass skylights.

"What is this place?" I asked, staring up at the dazzling ceiling.

"Subway stations used to be a lot fancier," Grayson said. "They closed this one back in the 1940s when the trains went from five to ten cars long. Ten-car trains are too long to fit in the curve."

"So they just left it empty?"

"It's called a ghost station," Natalie said. "There are ten in New York. This one's my favorite."

The flatline party took full advantage of the location. On one side of the tracks, zombies of all ages were socializing. There were some Level 3s hanging out on the fringes of the group, but most everyone looked like normal, everyday people. They certainly didn't look dangerous.

On the other side of the tracks was a long row of tables where merchants had set up shop. Strands of white lights hung from archway to archway, giving the whole station the look of an outdoor street festival or farmers' market.

"You're going to have to make it for thirty minutes on your own," Alex said.

Suddenly, I was overcome with panic. "You're not going to leave me here, are you?"

"Of course not," Natalie reassured me. "We'll stay close by and keep an eye on you."

"And if anything goes wrong, we'll step in," Grayson

added. "But the whole point is for you to pass yourself off as undead without any help."

"Remember the no-breathers policy?" Alex asked.

"How could I forget?"

He looked me in the eye. "They take that seriously. So be careful."

I nodded.

Just like that, they disappeared into the crowd and I was all alone. And here's the hard part. Even if everyone at this party was alive and it was being held in the courtyard of my apartment building, I'd still have trouble fitting in. Social situations baffle me. I never know what to say or do.

I figured I'd have a better shot dealing with the merchants, so I made my way to their side of the tracks. Most of them were selling items to solve problems specific to the undead.

I watched a man demonstrate a tiny but high-powered flashlight. He pointed it down the subway tunnel, and it illuminated much farther than I would have thought possible.

I couldn't help thinking that a light like that would have come in handy in the aqueduct. I was admiring it when a pair of hands suddenly grabbed my shoulders from behind. I tried to pull away, but the grip was too tight.

Then this unseen person leaned up and whispered into my ear, "Makeup like that won't get you too far."

I couldn't believe it. I hadn't even lasted fifteen minutes. I was trying to figure out an escape plan when she whispered something else.

"Come to my booth, and I'll show you how to pass for the living."

I looked over my shoulder and saw the smiling face of a woman who wore way too much makeup. She hadn't blown my cover at all. She was just trying to make a sale.

She led me to a table filled with homemade beauty supplies and tried to convince me that I just "had to have" some of her special lotions and creams. She called them Betty's Beauty Balms.

"Look at your hands," she said with mock terror. "There's no way you could pass those off as live human flesh. No offense."

"None taken," I replied, trying not to laugh.

"They're too pale," she explained. "But try a dab of this, and you'll see a miracle."

She scooped out a glob of coffee-colored cream and smeared it all over the back of my hand. Making it the same color as the Salinger sisters after one of their spray-on tanning sessions.

"See what I mean?" she said. "Now you almost look human."

"Almost," I said, still trying not to laugh. "Like you promised, it's a miracle."

"Great, so how many jars do you want to buy?" she asked hopefully. "Just ten dollars each."

"I'll have to think about it," I answered, trying to be polite. "Let me get back to you."

She went to show me something else, but I just turned away. I walked along the row of booths and stopped at a table where a man was selling something I thought should be in high demand in Dead City: toothpaste.

At least that's what I thought it was until he held up a tube and asked, "Hungry?"

I was confused until he squeezed a dollop of brown paste onto a plastic spoon and I realized that it was food. Or at least the undead version of food.

Alex and Natalie had both warned me about this. Unless they were trying to pass themselves off in front of the living, the undead didn't eat normal food. Instead, they usually ate a paste enriched with key vitamins and nutrients. They told me it wasn't harmful to the living, but since the undead had heightened senses of taste and smell, what was pleasing to them was not to us.

"Lots of calcium and vitamin D for your bones," he said, offering it to me. It was so unappetizing, it made cafeteria food look tasty. But I was worried that rejecting it might give me away.

I thought about the no-breathers policy and forced a smile. "Thanks. I'd love to try some."

My plan was to take it all in one big bite. I tried to suck it down quick enough to keep from actually tasting it, but that didn't work.

It tasted kind of like a big glob of wasabi I once ate by accident at a Japanese restaurant. As I forced myself to swallow it, I felt a burning sensation in my mouth and tears welling up in my eyes.

"Delicious, isn't it?" he asked.

I couldn't speak, so I just nodded and went, "Mmmm."

Fearful of what might have been waiting next, I bypassed all the other tables until I reached the end of the row. There, I came upon a guy who looked like he might be in college, giving a speech to anyone who would listen. He was bald and had a long scar that ran along his cheek and up to the top of his scalp. I wondered if it was the result of whatever had killed him. He passionately argued for the undead to stand up for their rights.

"Why should we hide underground like frightened

moles?" he demanded. "We did not choose to be this way. We did not ask to lose the sweet taste of fresh air and the warm comfort of sunlight against our skin. We have as much claim to this city as the living. We need to come together and march forward as a group with one voice, to confront those who scare us so."

"You'll certainly scare them back with that scar of yours," someone heckled him.

It didn't seem to bother him that no one was agreeing with him. Some of the people laughed, and a couple tried to goad him into an argument, but he just kept making his points. That's when I realized something.

He was absolutely right.

I thought back to the day the others had asked me to become an Omega. They said it was our responsibility to police *and* protect the undead. Training had focused a great deal on the policing part, but this trip to the flatline party and this speech had reminded me about the need to protect as well.

Most of the people at this party weren't dangerous to anyone. They just wanted to live in peace. Even if their version of living was different from what we're used to, it seemed like a fair request.

As others continued to give him a hard time, he looked

into the crowd for a friendly face, and he settled on mine.

"What about you? Do you think the living know more than we do?"

I thought about it for a second. "No," I answered honestly. "I think they know less than we do."

He cocked his head to the side, surprised by what I had said. "What do you mean?"

"They only know what it's like to be alive," I replied. "We know that too. But they have no idea what it's like not to be alive. That's something they'll never understand."

He smiled and nodded. "Absolutely. This one speaks the truth."

I was pleased . . . and a little freaked out. Not only was I able to pass myself off as undead (pleased), I was beginning to think that I might fit in better among them than among the living (freaked out).

Just then another hand grabbed my shoulder from behind. This time it wasn't a vendor. It was Alex.

"We told you to blend in," he said with a laugh. "Not stand out."

Natalie and Grayson walked up from the other side.

"You made it to thirty minutes," she said, pleased. "Let's get out of here before you wind up running for zombie council."

She laughed, and I could tell by their expressions that they were happy with how I had done.

"How do we get out?" I asked. "The same tunnel we used to get here?"

"Nah," Alex said. "We should go straight to the surface. I know a shortcut."

As we followed Alex, Grayson leaned toward me and whispered, "I liked what you said about the living and the undead. You're absolutely right."

Alex led us to one of the subway station's old stairwells. It was blocked off by a metal gate, which he managed to pry open a little.

"This should take us up to the street," he said.

We had to squeeze through the opening one at a time. I was the last one in our group, and there was a zombie right behind me using the same exit.

I smiled at him, but he didn't respond. If I had to guess, I would have said he was a Level 3, but I wasn't sure.

When it was my turn to squeeze past the gate, one of the metal links scratched a cut all along my forearm. It burned with pain, but I remembered not to cry out or make any pained expressions.

After all, only breathers feel pain.

What I wasn't able to control, unfortunately, was the

trickle of blood that started to run from my elbow to my wrist.

I looked back and saw the zombie staring first at the blood and then at me. Even in the darkness, there was no mistaking the orange-and-yellow glow of his teeth as he smiled and prepared to attack.

It's Time to Get My Zeke On

G uys, we've got a problem." I tried to sound calm, but the squeal of my voice was a dead giveaway that I was anything but.

Natalie was right in front of me. When she turned, she could see the blood on my arm and the look on the zombie's face. She yanked me through the gate and tried to slam it shut on the Level 3 killing machine before he could come after me.

"Get out! Get out!" she barked.

Natalie did her best to hold the gate closed while the rest of us started to run up the stairwell. The last thing we needed was a fight with a zombie at a flatline party. Considering we were outnumbered about four hundred to four, there was no way that could turn out well.

It's amazing how fast and strong you are when you're properly motivated. I was able to clear three steps at a time as we raced up the stairs to the next level. Unfortunately, when we got there, we ran into a dead end.

"I thought you said this was a shortcut," I wailed.

"You know, I may have been thinking about the ghost station over on Worth," Alex offered sheepishly. "I get them confused."

Seconds later, Natalie was barreling toward us.

"He's coming and he's unhappy!" she exclaimed. "We have got to move!"

She bolted out onto the mezzanine, and we were right behind her. I could hear the party going on below; luckily, they couldn't see us from where they were. We ran full speed toward an exit that led to the street.

The zombie, however, was amazingly fast. He caught up to us halfway across the mezzanine and managed to kick my ankle in midstride. Both of us crashed and skidded across the floor.

He was a little slower getting up, though, which gave the four of us enough time to surround him. He sat there for a moment, looking from person to person, trying to figure out what to do.

"Make sure no one followed us," Alex told Grayson.

"Got it," Grayson replied as he hurried over to the stairwell.

At this point I expected Alex to show off his skills and wipe the floor with this guy. Instead, he walked over to Natalie and then whispered to her. The zombie, meanwhile, slowly stood, and with everyone else suddenly busy, he began to size me up.

"Hey, guys," I said, trying to redirect their attention back to the situation. "You want to check this out?"

Grayson came back from the stairwell. "We're clear. It's just us."

The zombie was now striking a combat pose. He looked just like Alex did when we practiced martial arts at the YMCA. Only he had terrifying teeth and very angry eyes.

"Seriously, guys," I pleaded. "How about a little help here?"

Alex looked at me and smiled. "Nope."

I've got to say, that's not what I expected to hear.

"What do you mean, 'nope'?"

"You're on your own," he answered. "This will be the final portion of your exam."

I turned back toward the Level 3. He was full of hate, and he was about to attack.

"C'mon, guys," I begged. "Enough with the joking."

"We're not joking," Natalie said. "You can do this."

"Use what we've taught you," Grayson added. He made a clapping motion with his hands to remind me of CLAP. CLAP is the memory tool Omegas are taught for the proper procedure when confronting the undead. At a moment like this, it seemed a little . . . *inadequate*.

"CLAP?" I said, disbelieving. "Seriously?"

"It works," Grayson promised. "Go through the steps."

I scanned their faces, desperate to see a smile or a laugh, but when I saw their serious expressions, I realized I was going to have to fight this guy.

I turned back to the Level 3 and flashed a phony smile as I ran through CLAP in my head. *C is for "calm,"* I thought. The first thing an Omega is supposed to do is calm the situation.

"Hey," I said all friendly-like. "Let's start over. First of all, I want to apologize for my behavior. I should not have come to your flatline party. That's my bad. Totally on me. But now I've left the party, right? So the problem's solved. And I promise I won't come back."

He snorted and started to move toward me. I kept my distance by matching every step of his with a step backward.

"Besides, did you hear me in there? I gave a pretty strong argument *in favor* of the rights of the undead. I'm on your side. I want to be a friend."

I offered my hand in friendship. He moved toward it, but instead of shaking, he slapped me across the palm. It stung and instantly started to throb.

So much for *C*. It was time to move on to *L*. *L is for "listen."* An Omega is supposed to listen and try to understand what's causing the zombie's anger.

"Maybe 'friend' is too strong a word," I continued. "But I can see that you're upset. Why don't you tell me why, so we can work out a solution and settle this peacefully?"

He yelled something impossible to decipher as he charged me again. This time he was swinging wildly, and one swing slammed against my head and shoulder, knocking me to the floor.

"Level 3s aren't big talkers," Natalie advised from the sidelines. "Especially when it comes to their feelings. You might want to skip to the next step."

"Thanks so much," I said sarcastically as I stood up

and brushed the dust off my hands and legs. "Seriously."

"Glad to be of help," she shot back with equal sass.

A is for "avoidance." An Omega should do everything possible to avoid a physical confrontation.

"I can tell we're not going to be able to work this out," I said to the zombie. "So I'm going to leave."

I moved toward the exit, but he grabbed me from behind and slammed me against the wall. Pain shot through my body. I was hot and sweaty and not in the mood to take this anymore.

"Can I go to the last step now?" I asked as clearly as I could with my face pressed up against the tiled mosaic.

"Yes," Alex said. "Start with the first thing I taught you."

I pushed back from the wall and shoved the zombie away to create a little space between us. "Bad news, buddy," I said with as much attitude as I could muster. *"P is for 'punish.'"*

Alex's first lesson was simple: *Go for the head.*

The zombie came at me, and I delivered a punch right into his face. It caught him completely off guard and knocked him to the ground.

I should have finished him off then, but I didn't. The problem was that despite all my training, I had never been in a fight. I was used to pads and sportsmanship. This was all-out war, and I was being too polite.

Alex, Grayson, and Natalie continued to watch from the sidelines, offering nothing more than moral support as the zombie and I traded blows. I was using a combination of Jeet Kune Do, fencing, and everything that Alex had taught me.

The zombie was wild and undisciplined, which made it hard to fight him. He didn't land too many punches, but I couldn't predict how he was going to fight.

At one point he threw a punch at me. I was able to move out of the way and grab his arm. I held on to it tight and tried to do a judo throw. When I did, his arm literally came out of its socket and off his body.

As if it wasn't gross enough to have an actual severed arm in my hand, my teammates now found humor in the situation.

"I'd give you a hand," Grayson offered, "but it looks like you already have too many."

"Now *that* was funny," Natalie said with a laugh as she gave him a high five.

"Thanks," he said.

I tossed the arm at them, and they had to jump out of the way to keep from getting hit. I turned and then charged right at the zombie and threw a punch that broke through his rib cage and inside his chest.

When I pulled out my fist, it was dripping with purple-and-red goop that almost made me throw up. It was like the worst biology lab ever.

This, of course, brought only more laughter from my so-called teammates.

"Are you guys just going to sit there and laugh all night?" I snapped, a little peeved.

"That depends," Alex shot back. "Are you just going to keep goofing off? Or are you going to use what we've taught you?"

He was right. This zombie was a bad guy, and I was going way too easy on him.

"Seriously, how hard can it be to go for the head?" Natalie pointed out. "He's only got one arm."

The zombie moved toward me again, slime coming out of his chest and his arm socket. I thought back to my first class with Alex and the Jeet Kune Do move I had done to him.

I tried to move as fluidly as possible as I dipped down low, spun around, and popped up right next to him. He didn't have a chance. I delivered three quick punches to the head, and the zombie dropped like a rock.

I was stunned, unsure of what had just happened. But he wasn't moving. He was dead. My first instinct was to feel bad. I think Grayson was the one who realized this.

"Don't," he said to me. "Don't feel guilty for one second. He was bad. He was looking to hurt you, us, anyone who looked at him the wrong way."

"Yes, but . . ." I motioned toward the party as I tried to put my feelings into words. "I was just arguing for zombie rights."

"His existence and his behavior put all those good people in danger," continued Grayson. "You helped them today."

"He's right," Alex said. "That's what we have to do when they become dangerous."

I was too stunned to think through it all, but I knew they were right. He was bad and had to be stopped.

"We'd better go," Natalie said.

"What about cleanup?" I asked.

Grayson shook his head. "We don't clean up in Dead City. Down here the undead take care of their own."

"Yeah," Alex said, moving toward the exit. "Let's get out of here . . . Zeke."

At first I didn't catch it. Then I realized what he had called me.

I was no longer a trainee. I was a full-fledged Omega. And just like my mother before me, I had become a "zombie killer."

I was a Zeke!

Ω 11

I Get Called to the Principal's Office... and It's a Good Thing

Learning about the Omegas, going through weeks of intensive training, and traveling underground to defeat a Level 3 zombie in hand-to-hand mortal combat was pretty life-changing stuff. So it shouldn't have been a surprise when I went back to school the following Monday, everything was totally . . . the same.

It turns out the one drawback of having a supercool secret identity is that you have to keep it a secret. Becoming a Zeke can't make you popular if none of your classmates even know what a Zeke is.

But I didn't mind the lack of popularity so much. After

all these years, I was kind of used to it. Even the fact that nobody knew I'd been to Dead City and fought a zombie didn't bother me. The thing that was driving me crazy was the fact that *I* knew I had been to Dead City and fought a zombie and couldn't seem to get back there again.

Once the initial shock had worn off, I was ready for more. Except Omegas can't just go looking for trouble. Until we receive word there's a problem that needs to be solved, all we can do is wait.

Every morning before school I met up with Natalie, Alex, and Grayson to find out if we had an assignment. And every morning for the next few days the answer was no.

It was beyond frustrating.

Then one day I was in the middle of an English class discussion about *The Outsiders* (a great book once you get over the characters having names like Pony Boy and Soda Pop) when I got called down to the principal's office.

Dr. Gootman's office is . . . different. It's a converted cottage on the edge of campus. A hundred years ago, when this was all a hospital, the cottage was where the chief doctor lived. Today it still feels like a home, only now one that belongs to a mad scientist.

It's surrounded by gardens where he grows bizarre-looking flowers and vegetables as part of his crossbreeding experiments. Inside, the kitchen has been converted into a chemistry lab, and what once was the living room now holds his desk and a conference table.

"Ah, the fair Miss Bigelow," he said with a smile as I came through the door. "Until this morning, I wasn't aware you were part of this study group."

I had no idea what he was talking about until I saw Natalie, Alex, and Grayson seated at the table. Apparently, our Omega Team was calling itself a "study group."

"I just joined," I told him, unsure what, if anything, he might know about what we really were.

"An excellent choice," he said to Natalie as he motioned for me to sit with the others. "Natalie tells me that you are working on an experiment as part of a research project," he continued.

"That's right," said Natalie. "And while we would normally never ask to leave the campus during school hours, it's very time sensitive. There's been a change in the weather, and I'm afraid if we wait until later to collect the data, the experiment will be compromised."

He mulled this over for a moment. "Well, we can't have that, can we?" he said. "Are you certain it has to be now?"

Natalie didn't blink. "Yes, sir."

That was all the certainty he needed. "Then I'll inform

the dean and your teachers that you'll be back by fifth period."

"Yes," she said. "We should be able to do that."

"It wasn't a question," he corrected.

"Yes, sir," she said. "We'll be back by fifth period."

He handed Natalie four passes and gave us all a final stern look before heading out the door. "Makeup work will be done immediately."

We all agreed.

He kept up the tough guy act, but when he turned away from us, I could see his reflection in the mirror, and he had a sly smile. He'd said what he needed to say, but he also had our backs.

The final thing he said as he walked out the door was "Be careful."

I waited for the door to close before I turned to Natalie and queried, "Study group?"

"What was I supposed to call it?" she asked. "Zombie-hunting team?"

I laughed. "Does he know about the Omegas?"

"We've often wondered," Natalie said.

"He's been principal at MIST for as long as anyone can remember," Grayson added. "I think he must know something. But he doesn't ask."

"Yeah," Alex added with a laugh. "He didn't even make Nat describe her experiment."

"What would you have said?" Grayson asked.

"Something about weather and soil samples," she said with a flip of her hand.

Alex shook his head. "That would have been convincing."

"So, what's the real reason?" I asked. "Why are we leaving campus during school hours?"

All eyes turned to Natalie.

"It's our first assignment as a team," she said.

The Prime-O—or Prime Omega—is the only person who knows the identities of all active Omega Teams. He's the one who gives us our assignments.

"A hunt job?" Alex asked, referring to an assignment in which we'd track a zombie who was causing problems.

"Nope," she said. "Strictly research at this point. Three dead bodies were discovered in a park right here on Roosevelt Island."

Grayson had a confused look. "Aren't dead bodies more of a police thing than an us thing?"

"These bodies aren't your normal variety," she said cryptically. "According to the coroner on the scene, they had no blood and appear to have been dead for quite some time . . . like, years."

"Okay, that is a little weird," Alex said. "But it still doesn't sound like our line of work."

"Maybe you should look at the picture the Prime-O sent," Natalie added as she handed her phone to Alex. "The bodies were arranged in a very particular fashion."

Alex was surprised by what he saw. "Is that what I think it is?" he asked.

She nodded. "Yes."

Grayson looked at the picture and also nodded. "I guess it is an us thing."

Finally, the phone got to me. When I saw the picture, I couldn't believe my eyes.

The three bodies were arranged in the shape of a giant omega.

12

How to Set a Trap

Try to relax," Alex said as we followed the brick pathway that wraps around Roosevelt Island.

I was just about to lie and tell him I *was* relaxed when I realized he wasn't talking to me. I was so caught up in my excitement, I hadn't noticed that Natalie's hands were clenched into nervous fists or that she was taking long, fast strides like an Olympic speed walker.

"I am relaxed," she snapped in a voice so tense that Grayson actually laughed.

That's when it dawned on me that in addition to this being my first assignment as an Omega, it was also Natalie's first one as a team leader. Even though Alex is older, both he and Grayson had insisted that she take the position when the team's previous leader graduated last year.

"I'm serious," Alex said as he put a friendly hand on her shoulder. "We picked you for a reason. You're going to do great, but you need to relax."

She started to disagree again but caught herself and took a deep breath instead. She stayed quiet for a moment before she managed to smile and say, "Thanks."

I had never seen Natalie flustered before. You could tell her mind was racing in a million different directions.

"We're just supposed to do research at the crime scene, right?" Grayson said. "That should be easy enough."

"It should be," she said, thinking something over. "But I'm worried it might be a trap."

Both boys stopped for a moment to consider this.

"What makes you think that?" I asked.

"Whoever positioned those bodies into a giant Omega knows we have to come check it out," she explained. "Maybe the whole point is just to get us out there so that they can see who we are and figure out our identities."

"So while we think we're spying on them . . ." Alex started.

"They're actually spying on us," finished Natalie.

"Hadn't thought of that," Grayson said, impressed.

Alex smiled at her. "See what I mean? That's why we picked you. You're brilliant."

We stopped talking for a moment as we walked past a couple of old men who were casting their fishing lines into the East River. Then we rounded the corner, and the crime scene came into view.

We were right on the edge of a park that overlooked the water. On the other side of the park was an old wooden farmhouse that was now some sort of history museum. (I'd walked past it a million times and never paid any attention.) In the grass right in front of the house's porch, yellow police tape marked the area where the bodies had been found.

Needless to say, the discovery of three dead bodies in a public park had attracted a crowd. In addition to the police, there was a television news crew and some pockets of people who'd been passing by and stopped to find out what was going on.

"The crowd's good," Natalie said. "It should help us blend in."

"But what if it *is* a trap?" asked Grayson. "What should we do about that?"

Natalie thought for a moment, and then something

caught her attention: the fishermen. She looked at them and nodded.

"We set a trap of our own right back at them," she answered, getting some of the swagger back in her voice. "Molly and I will approach the scene and find out as much as we can. Maybe we'll even get lucky and there will be someone we know from the morgue. If there are any zombies in the crowd, they'll know we're there."

"Sounds like exactly what they want," Alex said. "What will Grayson and I be doing?"

"You'll be circling the crowd, looking for whoever's watching Molls and me. They'll see us, but they won't see you. You'll be able to see where they go."

I looked over at the fishermen and realized what had inspired her. "So we're bait?"

Natalie smiled. "Yeah."

"I like it."

"Sounds good," Alex said. "I'll start left, Grayson, you go right."

Alex and Grayson began circling the park and checking out the different groups of people. Natalie and I waited a moment, and then we walked right toward the middle of it all.

"Trap or not, someone is sending us a message," she

said. "Look for any clues that might tell us what it is."

I nodded.

We eavesdropped on the TV reporter as he broadcast, but didn't learn anything except how to be overly dramatic. "Action News reporter Brock Hampton reporting from Roosevelt Island, where three men met an unlucky fate . . ." (Personally, I thought "unlucky" was a bit of an understatement.) We also heard two detectives talking about shoe print evidence they had found.

"It doesn't make any sense," one of them said. "There were three sets of shoe prints, and each one matches a pair of shoes on one of the dead bodies."

"What's wrong with that?" asked the other.

"What about the guy who arranged the bodies?" the first one asked. "Where are his shoe prints?"

Natalie and I shared a look when we heard that. We both shook our heads as we tried to figure it out. He had a point.

There was no one left from the coroner's office. Apparently, they had already loaded up the bodies and were taking them back to the freezer at the morgue.

We were standing off to the side talking when Natalie got a text from Alex. She handed her phone to me so that I could read it too. It said YANKEES CAP. YELLOW JACKET. SOUTHSIDE COFFEE SHOP.

Our trap had worked. Alex discovered someone watching us.

"Be cool," Natalie whispered as we both casually looked toward the south side of the park. There we saw a woman in a baseball cap and yellow jacket standing by a coffee shop. The colors made her look a little like a bumblebee. Like many of the other lookers-on, she was taking a picture with her phone. But unlike the others, she wasn't taking a picture of the crime scene.

She was taking a picture of us.

She noticed us looking right at her and got spooked. She slipped the phone back into her jacket pocket and quickly began to walk away.

"Do we follow her?" I asked urgently.

"No," Natalie said. "That might be part of the trap. She spotted us but not Alex. He'll tail her and see where she goes."

Even though Natalie had predicted it, I was a little spooked by the fact that someone had been watching us. Suddenly, I felt paranoid about all the people gathered around the park and wondered if any others were spying on us. I turned to scan the people's faces, and that's when an idea hit me.

"What if it's a standpoint?" I asked.

"What?" answered Natalie.

"When we want to find a past Omega, we have to find a standpoint and look for an indicator," I said.

"Yeah," she said drily. "I'm pretty sure I'm the one who taught you that."

"A standpoint is an Omega symbol," I continued. "Maybe that's what the bodies were supposed to be. A standpoint we were certain to find."

Her eyes opened wide as she considered this. "That's . . . interesting," she said, warming to the idea. "The problem is, there's no way you're going to be able to actually stand on the point with all those policemen around. See how close you can get and start looking."

"Me?"

"Remember the bakery?" she said with a laugh. "You're better at it than any of us."

I smiled at the compliment.

Over the next ten minutes, I positioned myself in a couple of spots as close as I could get to where the bodies had been found, and looked for any sort of coded message or indicator.

"Any luck?" Natalie asked when we regrouped.

"No," I answered, discouraged. "Sorry."

"Don't be. It was a good idea. It still is. Maybe after all of this clears up, we can come back and look again."

Grayson and Alex were headed our way, and we walked over to meet them.

"Did you follow her?" Natalie asked.

"Did I follow her?" Alex replied, a little offended. "Of course I did. She was definitely undead. She was also pretty clever . . . and paranoid. I don't think she knew I was there, but she still used hard-core evasive techniques. She went down into Dead City by way of that old pumping station near the ruins."

"Well done," Natalie said. "We'll have to go back and check that out."

"I wasn't nearly as successful," Grayson said, shaking his head. "I didn't find any undead and I didn't learn anything when I poked around the Blackwell House."

It took a moment for the name to register.

"What's the Blackwell House?" I asked.

He gave me an "are you kidding me?" look.

"Haven't you ever noticed the two-story wooden farmhouse before?" he said, pointing at it. "You walk by it every day on the way to school."

"I've noticed it," I said. "But I didn't know what it was called."

Of course, Grayson being Grayson, he not only knew what it was called, but also its entire history. "It's one of the oldest houses in New York. The Blackwells built it right after the Revolutionary War, when this island was their farmland."

Natalie and I shared a look. Grayson had no idea that he'd discovered the key bit of evidence.

"What?" asked Alex.

"Yeah," added Grayson. "Why does the name of the farmhouse matter?"

We both said it at the same time: "Cornelius Blackwell!"

"Who's Cornelius Blackwell?" Grayson asked.

"A body that's missing from the Old Marble Cemetery," I said.

"And now three bodies turn up at the Blackwell House," Natalie continued. "That can't be a coincidence."

"Technically, it can," Alex said. "And even if it's not, how could you ever know for sure that Cornelius Blackwell is one of the bodies?"

"All we have to do is find out if any of them is missing his left ring finger," Natalie offered.

"Cool," I said, realizing she was right. I even gave her a fist bump. "We can pay a visit to the freezer and count some fingers."

"Absolutely," she answered.

We were happy, but the guys were completely confused. As we headed back to school, Natalie began to fill them in on what had happened when we went to the Old Marble Cemetery with Dr. Hidalgo. If the finger we'd found at the cemetery was from one of the bodies found here, we'd know for sure.

But then something caught my eye and stopped me in my tracks.

I held my hand up for Natalie to stop talking and asked, "How many numbers do they draw for the lottery?"

"Oh, don't ever play the lottery," Grayson said, shaking his head. "The odds of winning are less than the odds of—"

"I know that," I said, cutting him off. "I don't want to play it. I just want to know how many numbers they draw."

"Six," he answered.

"And how high do they go?"

"Sixty," Alex said.

"That's what I thought," I replied.

"Then what's the problem?" asked Alex.

"That."

I pointed to the window of the coffee shop. Earlier, when I'd been looking for an indicator, I couldn't see it because a tree was blocking my view. Now it was clear as day. And it was perfectly in line with where the bodies had been arranged.

It was a sign with the winning lottery numbers written on it. Only they couldn't have been the actual numbers because there were only four of them, and two of those were higher than sixty.

They were 4, 74, 18, 75.

It was the first Omega code I had learned in training.

"BEWARE!"

I Meet the One and Only Cornelius Blackwell

As we walked back to school, we tried to figure out the meaning of the "beware" message. I suggested the most obvious explanation.

"Someone's trying to warn us about something."

"Maybe," Alex said with a shrug. "But what? If they want to warn us, why be so mysterious? Why make us waste time trying to figure it out?"

Grayson considered this for a moment. "Maybe they want us to waste time," he reasoned. "Maybe they're not warning us at all. They're just trying to distract us from solving the real mystery—the one about the three bodies."

"Kind of like an *appel*," I said.

Grayson raised an eyebrow. "What's an *appel*?"

It wasn't very often that I knew something Grayson didn't, so I savored the moment.

"It's a fencing maneuver," I explained as I acted it out. "A fake out. You start to make a lunge, but instead of going through with it, you just stomp your lead foot. The motion and noise distract your opponent and create an opening so you can go in for the kill."

"That sounds ominous," Alex said.

"Worse than that," offered Natalie. "Because if it is some sort of fake out, it means one of the bad guys knows our code."

This troubling possibility quieted us as we thought about what might happen if a zombie could read our code.

Finally, Grayson broke the silence when we reached the campus. "Well, there is one thing we know for sure."

"What's that?"

He looked us each in the eye before answering, "That we need to be careful."

Natalie nodded. "You've got that right. Which is why I'm putting us on the buddy system. Until we know more, we go to and from school in pairs."

We all moaned.

The moans had nothing to do with not wanting to be together. The problem was that according to proper procedure, we would now have to meet up in alternate locations each morning. In my case, this meant I'd have to wake up about forty-five minutes earlier than usual.

"I don't want to hear it," Natalie said. "It's a safety issue."

"You're right," Alex agreed. "After school I'll go with Grayson and help write up our report for the Prime-O." All our messages to the Prime Omega had to be sent through Grayson's computer.

"Meanwhile," Natalie replied, "Molly and I will head over to the morgue to see if any of those bodies is missing a finger."

"Actually," I said sheepishly, "I have to go to fencing practice first."

Natalie gave me a "seriously?" look and the others laughed like they were in on a joke that I didn't know.

"I thought fencing was on Thursdays," she protested.

"We've got some tournaments coming up," I explained. "Coach Wilkes doubled our practice schedule."

Natalie took an exaggerated breath. "I guess that means I'll go watch Molly dance around with her little sword," she said as she did a goofy fencing impression. "And then we'll go to the morgue."

"It's not dancing," I declared defensively. "It's combat."

"Combat?" she said, having fun with it. "And what type of combat training are you doing today?"

I waited a moment before answering meekly, "We're practicing our footwork."

Everyone laughed, including me.

"Sounds like dancing to me," she called out as we split up and headed toward our fifth-period classes.

Despite the teasing, I knew they thought it was good for me to be on the fencing team. Not only was I learning how to use a sword, but more important, I was learning battle strategies.

For example, our footwork lesson that day centered on the *in quartata*. It's an evasive maneuver that requires you to step back and turn out of the way while simultaneously moving under your opponent's blade and into position to make a counterattack. The footwork is really tricky, and I was still running through it in my head after practice as Natalie and I rode the subway to the morgue.

"As I said," she joked, "it looks like dancing."

I looked down and realized that I wasn't just doing it in my head. I was actually going through the steps in the aisle of the subway car. "It's a cool move," I offered in my defense. "That is, it *would be* a cool move if I could figure out the footwork."

She pointed at my back leg. "You need to step back farther with your left foot, so that you can maintain better balance and counterthrust."

I couldn't believe my ears. I stopped and pointed an accusing finger. "You were on the fencing team?"

She laughed. "You obviously don't know my father. I couldn't *just* be on the fencing team. I had to have private lessons . . . a personal trainer . . . three weeks in Colorado Springs with the Olympic developmental team."

"Wow," I said, blown away. "How good are you?"

"*Were*, past tense," she answered. "I was good enough to get to the point that I hated every second of it. It finally got to be too much, and I burned out. I quit cold turkey last December. A little Christmas disappointment present for my dad."

"How'd he handle it?" I asked.

"The same way he always handles it when I let him down," she said with a combination of anger and embarrassment. "He refused to talk about it and ignored me just a little bit more than usual."

I had never heard her talk this way.

"My dad just says 'Don't get your eye poked out.'"

She smiled and looked almost envious. For the first time since I'd met her, it occurred to me that the fabulous life might not always be as fabulous as it looks. I dropped the subject, and we made small talk until we got to the morgue.

Considering it was after hours, we weren't sure how we were going to get downstairs and into the freezer to check out the dead bodies. I knew luck was on our side when I saw my favorite security guard working the main desk.

"I got this," I whispered to Natalie as we walked toward him.

"Good golly, Miss Molly," Jamaican Bob greeted me. *"Wagwan?"*

It had taken me most of one summer to figure out that *"Wagwan?"* is Jamaican slang for "What's going on?"

"Not much," I said, happy to see him. "What's going on with you?"

"Same old," he said.

"You remember Natalie, don't you?"

He gave me a wounded look. "As if I could forget her. How are you, Natalie?"

"I have too much homework, but other than that I'm doing great," she said with an easy smile.

So far, so good. But normally, this was when Bob would

tell one of his famously bad jokes. This time, though, there was no joke. There was just a question.

"What are you two doing here this time of day?"

It was more curious than suspicious, but I knew we had to be careful.

"We came by to see Dr. Hidalgo," I said, knowing full well that one of Dr. H's obsessive-compulsive habits was that he always left at precisely 5:45. "Is he still around?"

"He left about an hour ago," Bob said, giving me a skeptical look, as though he thought I should know the answer. "Same time as always."

"That's what I figured," I said, trying to cover. "We're supposed to pick up something for school, but fencing practice ran long."

"Fencing?" he said with a laugh. "You're taking fencing."

"Yeah," I said, happy that this had distracted him. "I'm on the school team and everything."

Now came the tricky part. I had to act like nothing was up, but still get us downstairs by ourselves.

"Since Dr. H isn't here, can you escort us to pick it up?" This drew a desperate look from Natalie, but I knew what I was doing. "It's down in the freezer."

That's why I knew I had him. No way would Bob go

near the freezer. Sure enough, he shook his head at the mere suggestion.

"Why don't you two just go by yourselves," he said as he waved us in. "The only way they're getting me in that room is when they wheel me in."

We put our book bags on the X-ray machine and walked through the metal detector. Just when I thought we were clear, he reached over and grabbed me by the wrist.

My heart jumped, but I tried to stay cool.

"One thing you should know," he said.

"What's that?" I asked with a gulp.

"Without you hanging around, it's been really *dead* around here." He let out a booming laugh, and I knew we were golden. Natalie and I both laughed with him as we grabbed our bags and disappeared down the hall.

"Nice work," Natalie said as we headed toward the stairs.

We went down three floors and made it to the door that led to the lab and freezer. I pulled the bottle of vanilla extract out of my backpack and swiped a finger of it under my nose. Natalie did the same.

"As if this place wasn't spooky enough during regular business hours," I said as we entered the lab.

A row of security lights flickering on the far wall gave the room an eerie green glow. I reached for the main switch, but Natalie stopped me.

"We don't want to advertise what we're doing," Natalie warned.

"Good point." Even in partial darkness, I knew every inch of the lab, inside and out. I went straight to the autopsy room and flicked on a small desk lamp while Natalie headed for the refrigerator.

"Here's the guest book," I said, picking up a ledger that listed the arrival and departure of every corpse that came through the office. I flipped it open to the page with the most recent entries.

"'Three John Does found on Roosevelt Island,'" I read aloud from the book. "They're in freezer drawers seven, eight, and nine."

"And look what I got from the fridge," Natalie said, holding up a little plastic bag and shaking it.

"I'm guessing it's a finger," I said with a smile.

"Don't forget the wedding ring," she added as we entered the freezer. We walked over to a wall of drawers. They're numbered from top to bottom, and the three we wanted to check were one on top of the other.

Natalie grabbed the handle to drawer number seven

and turned to me. "I'd like to introduce you to Mr. Cornelius Blackwell."

She pulled it open with great dramatic flair. But the moment was ruined when the drawer turned out to be empty. Natalie gave me an "okay, that's a little strange" expression. She tried the introduction again with drawer number eight.

"I'd like to introduce you to Mr. Cornelius Blackwell."

Drawer number eight was also empty.

So was nine. It was the Old Marble Cemetery all over again. You expect dead bodies, and then there aren't any.

"Are you sure you got those numbers right?" she asked me with an arched eyebrow.

"I'm positive," I said. "Check the cards."

Next to the handle of each drawer was a card with basic info about that particular body. Sure enough, all three drawers had cards that read "John Doe. Roosevelt Island."

Dr. Hidalgo pays close attention to every detail of his morgue. There's no way three bodies were not where they were supposed to be in the freezer.

"It just doesn't make any sense," Natalie said.

And it didn't make any sense . . . until we heard the loud crash coming from the next room.

14

Careful What You Wish For

The crash sounded like a bookcase tumbling over and spilling everything from its shelves. Our first reflex was to freeze, not because we were scared, but because we were the only ones on that floor and we worried that we had somehow caused it to happen. Then we heard another crash, followed by shattering glass, and realized that we weren't alone after all.

"Who is that?" I asked, in that way you whisper something you really want to scream.

Natalie considered it for a second before a look of realization came over her. She motioned to the empty drawers in front of us. "They're not dead. . . ." She pointed toward the noise and finished her thought. "They're undead."

Suddenly, it seemed so obvious.

"I think you're about to put your combat training to use," she continued.

The first thing that came to mind was how frustrated I had been that morning because we hadn't had any zombie action. I guess you should be careful what you wish for.

We each took a deep breath and nodded that we were ready. We moved silently from the freezer into the lab. The flickering security lights cast our shadows at odd angles across the examination tables.

The noise was coming from a small library, where Dr. H kept his medical books and journals. I remembered that the bookcases had locks on them, and it sounded as though someone without a key had decided to unlock them by smashing them to bits.

"There could be as many as three of them in there," Natalie reminded me. "They've got us outnumbered, but we've got surprise on our side."

"Surprise . . . and training," I said, trying to ease the tension and to reassure myself at the same time.

"And training," she agreed with a nod.

"Do we go in?" I asked, motioning toward the library door.

"No." She pointed to where she wanted me to stand, a spot about five feet from the door. "We let the fight come to us. We're going to wait for the door to open and then try to take control of the situation before they even know what hit them."

"Got it."

"You're ready for this, I know it," she reassured me. "But don't be afraid to ask for help if you need it."

"I won't," I promised.

From the sound of things, all the bookcases had now been pulled over, and someone (or up to three different someones) was digging through the rubble. After about thirty seconds the digging stopped, and we heard an inhuman laugh that sent chills down my spine.

"Brace yourself," Natalie whispered. "Here it comes."

My heart was racing so fast, I had to force myself to take short steady breaths to calm my nerves. A metallic taste filled my mouth as adrenaline rushed through my body.

The door flew open to reveal a giant man wearing one of the hospital gowns we drape over dead bodies while they await autopsy. The room was too dark to get a good look at him, but his eyes burned orange like coals in a fire, and he didn't seem the least bit bothered by the large chunks of glass sticking out of his cheek and forearm.

The light in the library allowed me a full view of the destruction behind him. More important, I could see that no one else was in there. As he stepped through the doorway, he held a book above his head triumphantly and started to call out with some sort of guttural wail.

I thought back to the *appel* maneuver from fencing and decided to try a modified version.

"He's alone!" I called out to Natalie as I jumped toward him and stomped my foot as loudly as I could.

He turned to look at me, and was too distracted to see her coming. Natalie ran right at him and delivered three rapid-fire kicks right into the side of his knee, crumpling him to the ground.

He bellowed and started yelling some sort of zombie gibberish. I didn't understand it, but I could tell he wasn't yelling at us.

He was calling for help.

His extreme height advantage was gone for as long as he writhed on the floor. It was the perfect chance for Natalie to finish him off with a solid kick to the face. But as she went to do it, she caught a glimmer of the green security light reflecting off the shards of glass in his cheek.

She stopped herself midkick in order to keep from cutting up her leg and foot.

This hesitation bought him enough time to get his bearings and stand up straight. Or at least as straight as you can stand with one of your legs bent at a forty-five-degree angle to the side.

He swung a fist and with it an armful of broken glass; Natalie easily ducked it. She countered with a flurry of punches to his stomach that sent him staggering back toward the library.

Watching her, I was mesmerized. She was amazingly tough and brave. I wondered if her "disappointed" father had any idea of what she was truly capable of.

I snapped out of it when I heard a crash behind us. I spun around to see another zombie in a hospital gown coming our way. Apparently, this group of undead was all from the *supersize* side of the menu, because he too was massive. Adding to his intimidating effect was the fact that one half of his head had wild red hair that tentacled in every direction while the other half had been completely shaved in preparation for his autopsy.

"I'll take care of this one," I called out to Natalie.

"Just remember there's another one around here somewhere," she said. "Quick kills are vital."

Easier said than done.

I could hear Natalie and Glass Face fighting behind me as I approached Big Red. I remembered the way Natalie had taunted the Level 3 in the subway station and how much it had frustrated him. I thought I'd give it a try.

"What's up with your haircut?" I asked, trying to sound cool and tough like the stars in those action movies my dad watches. "Did the barber have a half-off sale?"

Okay, so the joke didn't really work, but in my defense, it was my first day as an action hero. Being able to deliver cool lines in tense situations takes practice. Besides, I didn't really need to do anything to get him worked up. Turns out he was more than mad enough just at my being there.

He charged right at me, and I probably should have been more scared than I was. But while he had the size, I had the home-court advantage. This was *my* lab, and I knew everything in it!

I calmly grabbed the corner of a gurney, popped the wheel brake with my foot, and spun it around so that it was in front of me like a shopping cart.

I rammed it right at him as he charged at me, and we collided like two trains coming at each other on the same track. The force of it knocked me back onto my butt and cut him off at the waist so hard, he slammed face-first into the gurney.

I jumped up and then grabbed a large metal bowl Dr. H uses to hold human organs when he weighs them (I know, gross, but you get used to it), and I slammed it into the clean-shaven side of Big Red's head. I was hoping this would finish him off.

It didn't.

Instead, he stood up and swiped at the gurney with the back of his hand, sending it skittering off to the side. I could hear his neck bones crack into place as he cocked his head, side to side. Then he looked at me and my bowl and laughed.

(Okay, if you're ever looking for a scary Halloween costume, it turns out "giant laughing zombie with a half-shaved head in a hospital gown" is both inexpensive and effective.)

I held up my bowl like a weapon and refused to back down. As silly as it sounds, I thought if I could get another whack at his head with it, I might at least be able to daze him.

He charged at me again, and I instantly thought about fencing practice and the *in quartata* maneuver I had learned that day. This was the perfect situation: I'd turn out of his way, avoid him, and go from defense to offense with a lightning-quick blow to the back of his head.

At least, that's how I imagined it.

Unfortunately, I still couldn't get the footwork right, and I tripped over myself. Instead of the bowl against the back of his head, the only slamming was my nose and face against the concrete floor.

Big Red flipped me over, grabbed me by the shoulders, and picked me up like a doll. He lifted me all the way up, so that my eyes were even with his. Then he grossed me out by doing that thing where he sniffed me like a dog.

I cannot stress enough how much I hate that.

I squirmed and struggled but could not break loose. I had no idea what to do. Then I heard Natalie call out.

"What did I tell you about asking for help?" she said, frustrated.

"I know, but you looked kind of busy," I said, short of breath and struggling. "And I wanted to prove to you that I could take care of things myself."

"How's that working out?"

I squirmed some more, but still had no luck getting free. "Not so good."

"You might want to try a head butt," she suggested.

It wasn't exactly Jeet Kune Do, but it sounded like a

plan. I smiled and snapped my head forward, right into his face. Upside: It worked and he let go. Downside: It really hurt.

I slammed against the floor (again), and this time I didn't even bother getting up. I just used my small size to an advantage and started to scramble under the tables to get away from Big Red.

From my vantage point I could see Natalie was still going at it with Glass Face. His right leg was now barely attached below the knee, and it flopped around as he moved. Despite this, she hadn't been able to finish him. The broken glass was working like a booby trap in his face. As to fighting, he seemed more concerned with protecting the book than hurting her.

Suddenly all the lights came on, and I looked over at the door where Zombie Number Three had just flipped the switch. He was not quite as big as the others but was still plenty horrifying. He had changed from his hospital gown into street clothes and was carrying clothes for them as well. If I had to put my money on it, I'd say he was the brains of the operation.

He barked something at them, obviously upset they were wasting time fighting a couple of girls. Then he saw the book and smiled. He went straight for it.

Everything was different with the lights on. Especially because now the zombies could see all the equipment. The needles, scalpels, and blades that were normally just the tools of a medical examiner suddenly looked more like weapons. Big Red flashed a hideous orange-yellow smile as he grabbed two large blades from a table.

Zombie Number Three didn't care about us. He was only interested in the book. He snatched it from Glass Face and smiled broadly as he looked at the cover to see that they had the right one. As he held it, I got a good look at his hand and noticed something interesting.

He was missing his left ring finger.

I'd like to introduce you to Mr. Cornelius Blackwell.

He snapped at them again, and they turned their attention away from us and started to leave.

"The book," I pleaded with Natalie. "I don't know what it is. But we can't let them take it."

"You know some way to get them back?" she asked as she tried to catch her breath.

I looked down at the table and saw the answer in a little plastic bag.

"Hey, Corrrrneeeeliusss," I sang out. "Did you happen to lose a finger? And a wedding ring?"

He stopped and turned around. He looked right at me,

and I dangled the bag in the air. I even gave it an extra shake.

"We found this at the cemetery where you left it," I said. "I hope that wedding ring doesn't have any sentimental value for you. Especially with that sweet inscription from your wife and all. I can't decide if I want to melt it down, give it away, or just throw it in the river."

He was furious, which is exactly what I was hoping for.

"Or did you want it back?"

He started coming right at me, and when he got close, I tossed the bag onto the far side of the table I was next to. When he reached for it with his right hand, I grabbed a metal handsaw that Dr. H uses for (actually, you don't want to know what he uses it for, just know that he uses it) and with the best saber technique I knew, I chopped off his left hand at the wrist.

The hand, and more important, the book, fell to the floor. I grabbed them both (the hand was still kind of clutching the book) and raced toward the rear exit, snatching my backpack on the way.

As I ran, I pried the dead fingers off the book, which I then shoved into my bag. Natalie caught up with me at the door and we ran down the hallway. We made it around the corner and almost all the way to the stairs before we had to stop.

Big Red and Glass Face had beaten us there and were blocking our escape.

A few seconds later Cornelius Blackwell came out of the lab. He had the bag and the severed hand. And, understandably, he was in a pretty bad mood.

I turned to Natalie and finally took her advice.

"Help."

Big Zombies, Little Women

We were trapped. Glass Face and Big Red blocked the stairs and elevator while Cornelius Blackwell stood between us and the lab. To say that they were angry would be an understatement. I'd bashed in the side of Big Red's head, and thanks to Natalie, the lower half of Glass Face's left leg was now barely attached at the knee.

But the angriest was Blackwell.

Not only had I chopped off his hand, but I had also stolen the one thing he'd come to get. He approached us slowly, careful not to make any sudden movements. And while it was a struggle for him to form the word, I knew exactly what he was trying to say.

"Boooookkk."

"What book?" I answered, trying to play dumb. "I don't have any book."

He snarled and motioned to the others to start closing in. As they did, Natalie turned so that we were back-to-back, our shoulder blades pressed against each other, ready to fight in any direction. We'd almost run out of time when she cocked her head to the side and whispered the one word capable of bringing a smile to my face.

"Shortcut."

I knew exactly what she meant. The day he'd taken us to the Old Marble Cemetery, Dr. H had led us out of the morgue through a series of basement hallways. He'd called it his shortcut. Now it was our escape route.

First, though, we needed to distract the undead.

"Wait, wait," I said, holding up my hands for them to stop. "I have the book, and I'll give it to you. Just let me get it out."

They held their ground as I slipped the backpack off my shoulder and then unzipped it. I reached in and grabbed the biggest textbook I could find (*Advanced Biology*, hardcover edition), careful to make sure they couldn't see it. Then I looked right into the cold dead eyes of Cornelius Blackwell.

"Is this the one you mean?"

In one fluid motion I pulled out the book and swung it as hard as I could. I caught him squarely under the chin with an uppercut. He staggered backward, and that was all the opening we needed. We turned down the hall and started to sprint at full speed.

"Tell me you remember the way," I pleaded breathlessly.

"Just follow me," Natalie answered as she took the lead, a wild smile on her face.

Not once did I look back to see how close they were. All I did was run. We raced along the narrow hallways, through an old lab that reeked of formaldehyde, and up three mini-stairwells, fighting through the cobwebs, twisting and turning until we reached a door that opened onto First Avenue.

My immediate reaction was to suck in a lungful of fresh air and let out a sigh of relief.

"We're not safe yet," Natalie reminded me. "As soon as they get out of those hospital gowns and into street clothes, they'll be able to follow us anywhere in Manhattan. They have your scent.

"We need to get off the island," she continued. "Now!"

I looked for a cab but didn't see one. It defies all logic, but whenever you actually *need* a cab, they're nowhere to be found. If we didn't need one, they'd be everywhere.

Then I heard the sound of the zombies coming up from the basement, and my heart went into turbo drive.

"I know where we can go!" I blurted excitedly. "Alpha Bakery."

The bakery was only two blocks away. I knew that if we could make it there, we'd get help.

MIST doesn't have a track team, but if it did, Natalie and I would have qualified based solely on our sprint down First Ave. I don't think I've ever run that fast in my life.

When we finally burst into the bakery, we actually knocked the bell from above the doorway and sent it clanging across the floor. Luckily, there were no customers in the store. Only the baker, who was not particularly happy to see me so soon after his warning.

"What did I tell you about coming here without an *imminent need*?" he demanded, his big puffy cheeks red with frustration. But then he saw the panicked expressions on our faces and knew this was not another unnecessary visit.

This was real.

"This *is* an imminent need!" I declared. "We're being

chased by three massive zombies and need to get off the island right away."

Talk about sentences you never imagined yourself saying.

"Quick!" he replied urgently as he lifted a panel in the counter. "Hide in the pantry." We rushed through the opening and into the back of the store.

"Go in there and lock the door," he said, motioning to a small storage room. "Do not unlock it for *anyone* but me."

"How will we know it's you?" I asked as I tried to catch my breath.

"There's a monitor in there for the security cameras," he explained. "You'll be able to see everything in the bakery. Remember, no one but me."

"Got it!" we said in unison.

We rushed in and closed the door behind us. Natalie bolted the lock and then took a deep breath. She relaxed for a second (but only one) before she turned to me and angrily asked, "How come he recognized you? How come he'd talked to you before?"

I didn't have it in me to make up some elaborate excuse or explanation, so I went with the truth. "I broke the rules and came by the bakery. It was stupid, and I know that.

But can you get mad at me after this is over and we know we're still alive?"

There would be explaining to do later; for now she let it go and turned her attention to the monitor.

"Here they come," she said, pointing at the screen, which had images from four different cameras. On one we were able to see the zombies walking up the sidewalk, and on another we saw them as they entered the bakery. They tried to act normal, which was a bit ridiculous considering their appearance. They were colorful . . . even on a black-and-white screen.

Big Red had combed his hair across the bald half of his scalp. Or at least, he'd tried to. It kept flipping back over, so that now it looked like a giant *C* on the top of his head. Glass Face, meanwhile, had taken all the glass shards out of his cheek, so now he would be more accurately called Open Wound Face. He also tried not to limp too noticeably, but the lower part of his left leg kept dragging behind him at odd angles. Finally, Cornelius Blackwell did his best to mask his missing left hand by sticking his arm deep into his jacket pocket. It would have been funny if it weren't for the fact that they were trying to kill us.

And as if their bizarre appearance wasn't already

enough to attract attention, Big Red was sniffing the air like some sort of undead bloodhound hot on my scent. Despite all this, the baker acted like it was just a normal day and they were regular customers.

"Welcome!" he greeted them warmly. He winked at Big Red and offered, "I bet that's the vanilla you smell. Wonderful, isn't it? There's nothing more powerful to the nose than the smell of vanilla. *Nothing in the world.*"

Natalie nodded, smiling. "Brilliant!"

"What's brilliant?" I asked.

"He's talking to *us,*" she said as she started to search the shelves of the pantry. "He wants us to find vanilla. There's got to be some in here."

The pantry was filled with giant-sized containers of baking ingredients. Twenty-pound bags of sugar and flour were stacked up along one wall while shelves filled with cans of cinnamon, bags of chocolate chips, and boxes of sprinkles lined the others.

"Check it out," Natalie said as she crouched low. She'd found a row with gallon jugs of vanilla. "Triple-strength Madagascar pure vanilla concentrate." She looked up at me with a grin. "This should hide your scent perfectly."

"Great idea," I said with a shrug. "But how do you suppose we'll squirt it up his nose?"

She started to laugh. "That's not what I meant. Close your eyes tight, this could burn."

It still took a moment for me to realize that her plan was to cover my scent by covering *me* . . . with the vanilla.

"No way!" I objected. "You cannot be serious."

"Yes way! And I am."

"But I'll smell for days!"

"You don't have much of a choice," she said as she started to unscrew the cap. "Unless you'd rather smell like Dead City?"

"Well, if you're going to put it that way . . ."

If you've never worked in a bakery before, let me tell you that triple-strength Madagascar pure vanilla concentrate is as much syrup as it is liquid. It made a gurgling noise as Natalie poured it on top of my head. It slowly oozed through my hair, down my face, and, well, you get the picture.

It was pointless to fight, so I did my best to speed up the process by rubbing it in. My one lucky break was that I was still in the gym shorts and T-shirt I'd worn to fencing, so I wasn't ruining any clothes I cared about.

Natalie tried not to smile too much, but she failed miserably. I couldn't really blame her. When I saw my reflection in the stainless-steel door of the pantry, it took everything I had to keep from busting out.

"This is ridiculous," I whispered, trying not to crack up and make any noise that might attract attention.

Ridiculous . . . but also effective.

It wasn't long before the look on Big Red's face became even more confused than usual. He had clearly lost my scent. A minute later he motioned to the others, and the three of them left the bakery.

On the security monitor we saw them linger on the sidewalk, trying to catch a whiff of me. Once they were gone, the baker snuck us out in the back of his delivery truck. He drove to Queens, dropping us off right in front of my apartment building.

Face-to-face on the sidewalk, no longer in danger, the three of us looked at one another and smiled.

"It's been a while since I've done anything like this," he said, pleased to have a little taste of zombie action again. "I didn't realize how much I missed it. So tell me, did you two inflict all that damage? The broken leg? The missing hand?"

Natalie and I looked at each other and then at him. In unison we said, "Yeah."

"I love it," he said with a hearty laugh.

"Thanks for all the help," Natalie said.

"Omega today, Omega forever," he replied. "Anything else you need?"

"You got any tips on how to get rid of the smell of triple-strength Madagascar pure vanilla concentrate?" I asked hopefully.

"Showers, plural," he answered. "Lots and lots of showers."

He started toward his truck but stopped and turned back to us. He thought for a moment, trying to pick out the right words for what he wanted to say. "Molly . . . your mom . . . she was the best."

"Yeah," I said with a nod. "They say she was quite the Zeke."

"Yes, but that's not what I meant," he said, shaking his head. "She wasn't just the best zombie killer. She was the best . . . everything. The best *person* I ever knew. She'd be really proud of you."

A warm feeling came over me (although that could have been the vanilla settling into my pores) as I thought about her. Then I looked up at him. "Thanks."

Natalie and I hurried upstairs. My dad was hard at work in the kitchen. Luckily, the powerful aroma of his spaghetti sauce let me slip by unnoticed. Natalie hung out in my room while I took a quick shower.

Okay, maybe "quick" is not the right word. Despite scrubbing so hard that my skin turned bright pink and washing my hair three times, I still smelled like an ice cream factory. But at least all the sticky goop was off me.

When I walked into my room, I found Natalie sitting on the floor with the contents of my backpack spread out around her. She had a worried look on her face.

"Something wrong?" I asked.

"What happened to the book?" she replied, looking up at me.

"What do you mean? It was in my bag."

"No, it wasn't." She motioned to the piles around her. "They're all either textbooks or from the school library."

"That doesn't make any sense," I said, thoroughly confused. "I know I put it there, and they never got near my backpack. Besides, I don't have any library books. My card was revoked until next semester due to excessive overdue fines."

"Seriously?" she said, shooting me an incredulous look. "How hard is it to remember to return a book?"

"Apparently, harder than it sounds," I responded. "Now, do you mind not passing judgment? Just know that I don't have any library books."

"Well, then, what's this?"

She held up a medium-sized green book and turned it

so that I could read the stamp along the side: "Property of MIST Library."

"Well, I don't know why it was at the morgue," I said, "but that's the book they had. I never saw it before that scary zombie dude burst through the door and held it up in the air."

Natalie cracked a crooked smile as she shook her head. "Then something's really wrong here," she said. "Because it does not make sense that three zombies would climb out of their graves, stage an elaborate death scene, tear up the morgue, and fight to the death to get a copy of this."

She turned the book so that I could see the cover. And when I saw what it was, I had to agree that it didn't make any sense.

The book was *Little Women* by Louisa May Alcott.

Geek Mythology

As Natalie stood there holding the book, I tried to think of any reason why three zombies would be so desperate to get a copy of *Little Women*.

"Ever read it?" she asked me.

"Of course," I answered. "Haven't you?"

She shook her head. "Never interested me."

"Really? Not even in fifth grade?"

She laughed. "In fifth grade my favorite book was *Emerging Principles of Nanotechnology*." (Sometimes Natalie almost makes me feel normal by comparison.)

"Well, then, you've really missed out, because the

book is *sooooo* good. It's set in New England during the Civil War and is about four sisters who try to keep up their spirits despite hard times. They take care of their neighbors, go to parties, and put on plays for their friends and family."

"In other words," she answered, "it's the exact opposite of twenty-first-century killer zombies who live beneath Manhattan."

"Pretty much," I said. "So you've got to wonder why they'd go through so much trouble to get a copy of a book they could pick up at any bookstore."

"Well, it's not actually *Little Women*," Natalie said as she opened it to the title page. "That's just what it says on the cover. The full title is *Louisa May Alcott's Little Women, the Theatricals of Jo, Meg, Amy, and Beth March*, by Margaret Key."

She handed me the book, and I flipped through it. Sure enough, a writer named Margaret Key had written entire scripts based on the plays put on by the sisters in the novel.

"Okay, so what, then?" I asked, half joking and half trying to figure it out. "The three of them want to start performing girl plays for their friends down in Dead City?"

Just the thought of them dressing up as the sisters made me laugh out loud.

"Not exactly Shakespeare in the Park," she replied.

"I can tell you, though, who would have loved this book," I added as a happy memory danced through my head. "My mother was obsessed with *Little Women*. It was her all-time favorite novel. She even named my sister Beth after one of the sisters in the book."

I handed it back to Natalie, and she flipped through it some more.

"I get that your mom would have liked it," Natalie replied, "but not why Cornelius Blackwell was so desperate to get his hand on it." She gave me a little wink and a smirk. "Notice I said *hand*—as in only one?"

"I *had* to chop it off," I said defensively. "It was the only way to get the book."

"And you're sure this is the book you pried from the fingers of that severed hand?" she asked, holding it up by the corner as if it suddenly had cooties.

"Positive," I said, replaying the gory scene in my head. "And I specifically remember that he checked the cover to make sure he had the right book. This is what they were after."

She thought about it for a second. "Now that you say that, I remember him checking it too."

We sat there dumbfounded, trying to think of any reasonable explanation and coming up with exactly zero.

"Okay, let's forget for a minute why they wanted it," I suggested, "and try to figure out what a book from the MIST school library was doing in the New York City morgue."

"Change of perspective. Good idea."

We mulled this over for a minute, and then Natalie made that "eureka" face she gets when she comes up with a brilliant idea.

She flipped to the back of the book and carefully slid the library return receipt from the pocket inside the cover. It was brittle and faded, but when she held it up to the light, she could still make out the faint writing. She read it and then laughed. "I know one thing the morgue and MIST have in common."

"What?" I asked eagerly.

"Apparently, you're not the only one in the family who's lousy at returning library books."

Now I realized what MIST had in common with the morgue. "You can't be serious."

"Oh, yeah," she said as she handed the slip to me.

I checked the slip and could not believe my eyes. The book was last checked out nearly thirty years earlier by a

MIST student named Rosemary Collins. My mother.

"You were right when you said your mom would have loved this book. She loved it so much, she checked it out and never returned it."

That's when the doorbell rang.

"I bet that's the boys," Natalie said. "I texted them from the delivery truck and a couple more times when you were in the shower. You were in there for a while."

Sure enough, Alex and Grayson were at the door, relieved to see us healthy and whole. Before we could fill them in on our adventure, my dad popped out from the kitchen.

"Hey, Molly, want to introduce me to your friends?"

"Sure thing, Dad. This is Natalie, Alex, and Grayson. We're working together on a research project for school."

"Nice to meet you all," he said. "I'm making baked rigatoni for dinner, if any of you would like to join us."

Alex, ever the food monster, smiled gleefully. "Is it true that you were selected the best cook in the entire New York City Fire Department?"

Dad, almost embarrassed, nodded. "I don't know how tough the competition was, but yes."

"Then I, for one, would very much like to have baked rigatoni."

"Me too," added Grayson.

All eyes turned to Natalie.

"Do you have enough for three extra people?" she asked sheepishly.

"More than enough," he answered with a smile. "I'll call you when it's ready."

I could tell Dad was thrilled at the prospect of other kids visiting. I think I've made it pretty clear that I'm not exactly a social butterfly (let's be honest, I'm not even a social caterpillar), and whatever friends Beth has, she tends to meet up with them away from home.

Dad went back into the kitchen while we headed to my room. Natalie and I filled the guys in on what happened at the morgue, our escape by way of the bakery, and our utter confusion about the book. That's when Alex caught us all by surprise by announcing, "*Little Women* rocks!"

"Are you serious?" Grayson asked incredulously. "You've actually read it?"

"Multiple times," Alex answered, without a hint of sarcasm or shame. "I have three younger sisters, and I read it to each one when they were little. I even did different voices for the characters. My Jo . . . off the charts."

"If you know it so well, maybe you can figure out why they wanted it," Natalie suggested as she tossed the book to him. "'Cause we sure can't."

Alex opened the book to the table of contents and then flashed a smile that up until that point I had seen him use only while looking at food.

"What a great idea," he said as he read through the play titles. "There's *The Witch's Curse*, that's the one where they perform on Christmas at the start of the book, *The Captive of Castile*, *The Greek Slave* . . ."

His voice trailed off as he continued down the list.

"What's wrong?" Natalie asked.

"Well . . . some of these aren't from the book at all."

"Really?" I asked.

"Like this one," he said. *"Atlas and Prometheus."*

"Now *that* sounds good," Grayson said, suddenly interested in the conversation.

"What do you mean?" asked Natalie.

"I may not know anything about *Little Women*," he answered, "but I know almost everything about Greek mythology."

"You sure you don't mean geek mythology?" Alex asked with a laugh.

"Call it what you want. I used to read myths to my little brothers at bedtime. I even did voices. My Hephaestus would put your Jo to shame."

We all laughed at that.

"Why would there be a play about Atlas and Prometheus in this book," Natalie wondered, "if it's not in the original?"

"Maybe there's something in the myth," I suggested. "What's it about?"

"Atlas and Prometheus were Titans, and they were brothers," Grayson replied. "But when the Titans went to war with the Olympians, Prometheus went against his own kind."

"All right," Natalie said, nodding. "Do you think that might have something to do with three Level 3 goons?"

Grayson shook his head. "Nothing I can think of."

As we looked further into the book, we discovered that most of the plays were not, in fact, from *Little Women*. Despite this, Margaret Key had written them as though they were. Each one featured the four sisters and was written in Louisa May Alcott's style.

We were stumped, staring off into space and trying to figure it out, when my father entered.

"Dinner's almost ready—" he said, before stopping himself and laughing at the perplexed looks on our faces. "Homework's that hard, huh?"

"Yeah," I answered.

"I don't suppose you know anything special about Atlas and Prometheus," joked Alex.

"Just the obvious," my dad said with a shrug, as if we all should know what he meant.

"What's 'the obvious'?" I asked.

"You really don't know?"

"No."

"What kind of New Yorkers are you?" he asked. "Atlas and Prometheus are the two giant statues at Rockefeller Center. Atlas is across the street from St. Patrick's."

"And Prometheus is right in front of the ice-skating rink," Grayson finished. "How did I miss that?"

"Yeah, how'd you miss that?" Alex asked, with a friendly toss of a pillow.

"There's a big statue out in the harbor, too," Dad joked. "Tall lady with a crown and a torch. I think her name may be Something Liberty."

"Very funny, Dad."

"Anyway," he said, with a clap of his hands, "dinner's in about half an hour."

He walked back toward the kitchen, and we turned to one another, our minds digesting this new information.

"Do you think it's a coincidence?" Natalie asked. "Or do you think the play actually has something to do with Rockefeller Center?"

"Let me see the book again." Alex picked it up and turned to the first scene of the play. He stared at it as if something might jump off the page and catch his attention. It took a moment, but something did, and a smile slowly began to form. "That's interesting."

"What?"

"Come here and look at the heading on the script," he said. He motioned to all of us, so we crowded next to him and scrunched together. "Read the top three lines."

PERFORMERS: JO, MEG, AMY, BETH

LOCALES: ZEUS'S HIDDEN APPLE ORCHARD,

TARTARUS, THE CHAMBER OF IAPEDUS

"So?" Natalie asked. "Is something wrong?"

"Not that I can see," added Grayson. "The locations are all from the classic myth."

Alex smiled. "Watch what happens when I cover the edges."

He pressed his hands down flat on the page so that they covered the edges.

"Now read it."

Suddenly a new phrase was visible in the middle.

O MEG A 'S HIDDEN CHAMBER

"Omega's hidden chamber?" I said, stunned.

Alex nodded. "I don't think this is a play. I think it's a code."

17

Book of Secrets

We scoured the book, looking for any possible connections to New York, zombies, or the Omegas and discovered something interesting in a Christmas play called *A Present from St. Nicholas*. In the story, Santa Claus brings a toy to a lonely prince named Belvedere. At first glance, it couldn't have less to do with the undead.

But hidden in the script, we found clues about St. Nicholas Heights, which is where City College is located, and Belvedere Castle, a European castle in the story, but also the name of a building in Central Park.

Still, other than the fact that they are both in New York, we couldn't come up with a connection between the college and the castle until Grayson found it online.

"Here's one thing they have in common," he announced while looking at a website about historic landmarks in the city. "They were both built from the same material."

"Gee, let me guess," I joked. "Bricks?"

"No," he answered, shaking his head. "They're both made entirely from Manhattan schist."

Alex gave him a look. "Seriously?"

Natalie was reading over Grayson's shoulder and noticed something else. "Here's another building made from Manhattan schist," she said. "The Sea and Land Church, down on the Lower East Side."

"And . . . ?" asked Alex, unsure of where this was leading.

"Listen to this." She picked up the book and read one of Belvedere's lines from the script. "'Oh, Saint Nicholas, I have searched my kingdom for this toy all along the *East Side*, across *Sea and Land*.'"

It began to make sense why the undead were so interested in the book.

"What *is* all this?" Natalie said, flipping through the pages.

Grayson took it from her and held it. "To maintain

secrecy, virtually everything we know about the Omegas and the undead has been passed down orally," he offered. "In fact, the only written records we know about are the *Book of the Dead*, which contains all the census information we collect, and the *Book of Secrets*."

"You guys told me about the *Book of the Dead* during training," I said. "But nobody said a thing about the *Book of Secrets*."

"That's because none of us really knows anything about it," Alex explained. "We don't even know for sure it exists. It may just be a rumor passed down from generation to generation."

"Supposedly," Natalie continued, "it contains codes and clues that lead you to a place where you can find the names of all Omegas, past and present, locations of hidden records and information, and even a doomsday plan to eliminate the entire undead population in case of an emergency."

I looked at Grayson. "And now you think *The Theatricals of Jo, Meg, Amy, and Beth March* is a third book that nobody knew about?"

"No," he answered as he held it up. "I think *it* is the *Book of Secrets*. It would be a classic Omega trick to hide it in plain sight right there in the MIST library."

We were all quiet for a moment as we considered the seriousness of what he was saying.

"I think so too," Natalie agreed. "And for some reason, your mother thought it needed to be moved out of the library, so she took it and eventually hid it in the morgue for safekeeping."

We all turned to Alex, who had taken the book from Grayson and was looking at its spine.

"What do you think?" Grayson asked him.

"I think the answer is right here in the Dewey decimal number from the library," he said. He turned it so we all could read the spine.

812.31

KEY

If you look in your local library, you'll see that 812.31 is right in the heart of the drama section. But if you look at the periodic table, you'll also see that it's a coded message: 8 stands for oxygen (O), 12 is magnesium (MG), and 31 is gallium (GA). All strung together it reads:

OMGGA

KEY

"Omega key," Alex said. "The key to all the Omega codes and secrets. I think we've only scratched the surface of what's inside here."

"Then we need to stop looking right now," Natalie said, taking charge again. "Whatever this is, we're not supposed to know about it. Grayson, when you get home tonight, send an emergency message to the Prime Omega. The Prime-O will tell us what to do."

Before she could say anything else, Dad called, "Dinner!" Further planning would have to wait.

Dinner was great. As expected, Dad's rigatoni was a huge hit. Less expected, Beth was actually nice to all my friends. Of course, that may have been because she thought Alex was cute. Then, about halfway through the meal, there was a knock on the door.

"Another guest?" Dad laughed as he got up to answer it. "Suddenly, we have the most popular apartment in the building."

"Word must have gotten out about your rigatoni," Alex mumbled, his mouth full of pasta.

At first I was surprised to see Dr. Hidalgo, but then it kind of made sense. I'd begun to suspect that in addition to being friends and coworkers, Dr. H and my mother had been Omegas together when they were at MIST. This kind of confirmed it. He may have given my dad some excuse about being in the neighborhood and wanting to say hello, but I knew he was there to make sure Natalie and I were all right.

"Alex, Grayson," I said, handling the introductions, "this is Dr. Hidalgo. Natalie and I interned for him down at the morgue. Well, technically, Natalie interned and I was just hanging around . . . you know . . . because I'm weird."

Everyone laughed.

"Nice to meet you both," he said, shaking their hands. Then he turned to me and Nat. "And very nice to see you two looking so well."

He closed his eyes for a second and let out a sigh of relief now that he'd found us safe and sound.

At my dad's insistence, he sat down and joined us for the rest of the meal. It reminded me of the lunch at Carmine's that Dr. H, Natalie, and I had after my adventure into the Blackwell crypt at the cemetery.

"By the way," he said, turning to me. "I was having trouble finding one of my books down at the morgue and wondered if it might have ended up with you by some chance."

I shot a quick look at the others. "I think I know the book you mean," I answered. "It's in my room."

He let out another sigh of relief, and it occurred to me that Dr. H might not be just any Omega. Maybe he was the Prime Omega, which would explain why he had the *Book of Secrets*.

After dinner I gave Dr. Hidalgo the copy of *Little Women*, and he clutched it tightly.

"Natalie and you really saved the day," he said with a mix of pride and appreciation. "You can't imagine how bad it would have been if they'd gotten this. But there's something more that I need from all four of you."

"Anything," I answered.

"Whatever you know, or think you know, or imagine you know about this book," he said, holding it up, "you need to forget. Completely."

I nodded. "Yes, sir."

"You can't just say it," he responded with total seriousness. "You have to mean it. This is for everyone's safety, especially yours. You have to promise me."

"I promise."

And when I said it, I really did mean it. But when I went back to my room, I found something that I could *not* forget.

Earlier, when I'd been in the shower and Natalie was looking for the book, she had dumped everything out of my backpack. Once dinner was over and everyone had gone home, I started sorting through the papers and putting them back where they belonged.

That's when I found the envelope.

My guess is that it must have fallen out of the *Book of Secrets* somewhere between the morgue and our apartment. I instantly recognized my mother's handwriting on the front, where she'd written: 92, 7, 71, 6, 19, 39 Al.

Using the periodic table code it spelled out "Unlucky 13." I know a lot of people think thirteen is an unlucky number. My mother wasn't one of them.

I could feel photographs inside the envelope. Since I couldn't be a hundred percent sure that the pictures were related to the *Book of Secrets*, I wouldn't technically be breaking my promise to Dr. H if I looked.

There were eight pictures in all. Each one had a number and a date written on the back. According to the dates, they had been taken over a period of nearly twenty years.

I didn't recognize anyone until photo number four. It was none other than Cornelius Blackwell, fat and happy, with his fingers and hand still attached. Two pictures later I came across Big Red. But the real surprise was the last picture.

It was a photograph of a man getting into a cab. And

even though it was taken from across the street and he was looking to the side, I recognized him instantly.

It was the man who had stolen my mom's purse and chased us up to the top of that building where we got locked on the roof for the night.

I had always assumed he was just some crazy person and it was a random robbery. Now I wasn't so sure. Why did my mother have a picture of him? And why would she keep it in the *Book of Secrets*? What if he was like Cornelius and Big Red? What if he was a zombie too?

That would explain why she tried to escape him by running up toward the roof. And if he was a zombie, maybe it wasn't random. Maybe he was targeting her.

He certainly didn't look crazy in this picture. He wore a suit and carried a briefcase.

Despite my promise to Dr. H, there would be no way for me to forget this. More important, there would be no way for me not to search for the answers to my questions.

And since I couldn't ask my mom or the other Omegas, there was only one way.

I would have to go back to Dead City.

Alone.

Party Crasher

Over the next few days, I debated whether or not I could really go through with my plan. The idea was to go down into Dead City, crash a flatline party, and show the picture around to see if anyone recognized the creepy guy who had tormented my mother and me.

It sounded simple enough, but it had some major design flaws.

First of all, I wasn't just breaking one of the rules. I was breaking the biggest rule of all. Omegas are only allowed to go into Dead City in groups of three or more. There are no exceptions. But I couldn't ask the others to come with me. We had specifically been instructed to ignore everything about the *Book of Secrets*. Asking them would mean putting them in the unfair position of having to choose between helping me and following the rules.

And since I couldn't ask anyone, I couldn't tell anyone either. When an Omega Team goes underground, they're supposed to notify the Prime-O. Not quite sure how I could have worded that one.

Dear Prime-O,
I'm doing something I'm not allowed to do and investigating something I'm not supposed to know about. Just thought you should know.
Love,
Molly

Needless to say, I didn't send a note. This meant that if something happened to me while I was down there, no one would know where to look. I wouldn't even be able to call or text for help because there's no cell service that far underground.

I was an army of one.

That Saturday afternoon my dad was working and my

sister was off doing whatever it is that popular kids do on weekends. This gave me the perfect opportunity to go into her room and raid her makeup drawer.

I didn't have three people to help me look like a walking corpse as I did at my first flatline party. So I started digging around and experimenting with Beth's extensive cosmetics collection all on my own.

Let's just say there was a learning curve.

I put on some powder that I thought would make me look pale, but mostly it just made me look like a pancake. And then, when I tried to use a mascara brush, I almost poked my eye out . . . twice.

Finally, as if things weren't going badly enough, I was staring at a tube of something called stick foundation, trying to figure out what the heck it was, when the door opened behind me.

"What do you think you're doing?"

I looked up at the mirror and saw the reflection of my sister looming in the doorway. She had the same expression she uses when she catches me trying to borrow her clothes.

"I'm putting on makeup," I offered lamely as I turned to face her.

I was ready for her to explode at me for being in her room and touching her stuff. But that's not what happened. Instead, she just kind of smiled and said, "Well, you're doing it . . . wrong. Very, very wrong."

She disappeared into the hallway, and I stood there frozen, unsure what I should do. I wondered if maybe she was looking for a camera so she could document the evidence of my invasion to show our father later. Instead, I heard her turn on a faucet for a moment.

When she came back into the room, she was carrying a damp washcloth.

"You going to hit me with that?" I asked, both confused and a little worried.

"Yes, because I'm that big a monster," she said, shaking her head. "Just clean off your face so we can start over."

She handed me the washcloth, and I began wiping off all the powder and mascara.

"You should have asked me," she said, motioning to her makeup drawer.

"I know," I answered. "I shouldn't have gone into your room without your permission."

"Well, that too," she said. "But I mean you should have asked me to help you with the makeup. I may be useless when it comes to molecular biology homework, but makeup is kind of in my wheelhouse."

It finally dawned on me that she really wasn't mad.

"You mean you'll show me how to do it?"

"Just like Mom showed me."

Over the next thirty minutes, Beth tutored me in the fine art of makeup for beginners. Granted, these were not the kind of lessons you need when you're trying to look like a corpse, but I didn't care. She had never talked to me this way, and it felt great.

"First of all," she told me, "you don't want to use too much. You're too young and pretty for that. Just a little accent here and there."

I turned and looked at her, totally dumbfounded. "You think I'm pretty?"

"It doesn't change the fact that you're a total freak who steals my clothes," she said. "But yes. And when you fully grow into your looks . . . watch out."

I was stunned.

She took out the stick foundation and drew a little line on each of my cheeks. "Rub this in until it's all smooth and the color blends. It will give your skin a slight glow and will hold the rest of the makeup in place."

"Foundation," I said, finally getting it. "Like how the foundation of a building holds its superstructure in place."

"Yeah," she said with a tilt of her head. "But let's not turn this into an engineering discussion."

"Got it."

I rubbed it in, and she watched closely to make sure I was doing it right.

"That's good," she said, nodding. "Now for a little eye shadow."

She flipped open a tray that looked like a watercolor kit and then dabbed a brush into a light brown shade. "Now close one eye and gently brush this on the lid."

"Like this?" I asked as I tried it.

"Gentle. You don't want to rub it in," she instructed. "Now try the other eye."

She watched me for a moment and then totally caught me off guard when she said, "I used to be so jealous of those eyes."

"Really? Why?"

"Are you kidding? Look at them." She pointed to my reflection in the mirror. "Not only do they look amazing, but they were just one more thing you had in common with Mom. One more thing that made you Mini-Mom. It wasn't enough you were a little brainiac like her. You had to have her eyes, too."

I was quiet for a moment. "Sorry."

"Don't be. I got over it a long time ago. Now I like them. I see them, and they remind me of her."

She handed me another brush.

"Put that in the outer corner of each eye,"

I started applying it on my left eye.

"Now you're getting it," she said as she nodded. "That's real good."

"I know a secret about you," I said cryptically as I began applying shadow to the other eye.

"Because you've been digging around in my room?"

"No," I answered. "Because I know what I know."

She looked at me, waiting to hear what it was. I made her sweat it out.

"Okay, so what's the secret?" she asked.

I stopped again and looked at her. "You're a brainiac too."

She almost looked like she was going to smile, but she swallowed it. I went back to brushing on the eye shadow.

"You try to hide it from everybody, especially the Salinger sisters, but I know what kind of grades you make. And I've read some of your English papers. They're amazing. You are such a good writer."

I put down the brush to signal that I was done.

"So *I'm* smart and *you're* pretty," she said as she checked to see how it looked.

I cracked a sly smile. "I won't tell if you don't."

"Deal," she said with a laugh. "By the way, it looks good."

I don't know if it was the makeup or just the confidence boost from what she said, but I liked the way I looked too. Unfortunately, I was supposed to look like a corpse. Still, it was a nice feeling.

I left the house and headed straight for J. Hood Wright Park. Like the last time, I was looking for some zombies who I could follow to a flatline party. This time the zombies found me first.

They were three girls in their early twenties, and with the exception of a few clues—such as the color of their teeth and the fact that two of them were wearing gloves to hide their skin—they looked totally normal. I wasn't even sure they were undead until one of them spoke up.

"I remember you," she said.

I was worried, but she was smiling, so I just went with the flow. "You do?"

"From the party about a month ago," she said. "You were the only one who agreed with Liberty."

I had no idea what she was talking about.

"Who's Liberty?"

"The crazy bald guy with the big scar," she said. "He goes to every flatline party and argues for equal rights for the undead. He was desperate, and you helped him out."

She laughed, and I wasn't sure how to react. Was she teasing me? Maybe she thought I was crazy too.

"It was cool," she added.

"Really?"

"Yeah," she said with a nod. "You want to go down with us?"

"Sure. That would be great."

I walked over and joined them. One of the other girls looked at me and smiled.

"Your makeup looks great," she said. "I'd never guess you were undead."

"I could never do it alone," I answered honestly. "My sister helped. She's amazing."

The third girl chimed in. "Well, maybe you can get her to help me, because my skin's beginning to look like those old paintings in museums."

"Haven't you tried Betty's Beauty Balms?" I joked, referring to the lame zombie makeup at the last party. They all laughed, and just like that, I was accepted—more than I ever had been by the girls in school.

I was tempted to flash the picture right there. If one of them recognized him, I wouldn't even have to go into Dead City. But I was worried that it might seem suspicious and give me away. So I just did my best to keep up with the conversation. About ten minutes later, a man came up to us and told us the location of the party.

"Abandoned steam tunnel underneath City College," he said. "Do you know it?"

The other girls nodded, so I did too.

My first thought was that City College was mentioned in the *Book of Secrets*. The main buildings were built entirely out of Manhattan schist. I wondered if that had something to do with why the party was there.

This party was much easier to get to than the last one. There were no long tunnels to tromp through and no water to fall into. We stayed aboveground until we reached the campus, where we went into an old maintenance building.

The girl who had recognized me led the way as we snuck into the building and went down into the lowest basement. It was so damp, my hair began to frizz the second we walked in. We bent down and practically crawled under a series of pipes. I was careful not to touch them because I could tell they were hot, and I didn't want to yelp and give myself away.

When we stood up again, we were in an abandoned tunnel underneath the college. It was filled with pipes that no longer carried steam. We followed them for about a block until we reached the party.

It was smaller than the last one but had the same feel. There were vendors lined up against the wall and people socializing wherever they could find space. I stayed with the three girls for a while, and then I went out into the crowd.

I showed the picture to three different people, telling them I was looking for an old friend of my mother's and wondering if they recognized him.

There is a secretive nature to the undead. Even the girls I walked with to the party never offered their names or asked for mine. And it was clear none of these people liked being asked to identify the picture. Each said they didn't know him and instantly moved on.

I was just about to approach a cluster of four women when a man came up behind me.

"You need to stop," he said.

I turned around and recognized him in an instant. It was the man they called Liberty—the one who believed in undead rights.

I smiled when I saw him.

"Hi," I said, with genuine friendliness.

He didn't return the sentiment.

"Did you mean what you said?" he asked me.

"What are you talking about?"

"When you said that the undead deserved rights? Did you mean that?"

"Of course," I answered. "If we don't get our right—"

He cut me off.

"I'm going to ask you again, *breather*," he said, using undead slang for the living. "Did you mean it?"

I was busted. I decided my best strategy was to be completely honest.

"I meant every word."

He looked deep in my eyes, trying to see if I was telling the truth.

"Then you'd better follow me," he said. "Because you're in real danger."

The Wildest Ride in Manhattan

I stood there staring at him, trying to process what he'd just said. I may have blinked, but if so, that was the only movement I was capable of. Beyond that, I was frozen with fear.

"I'm sorry. Could you repeat that?"

"I said you'd better follow me, because you're in real danger."

"And by real danger, you mean . . ."

"The kind that gives Dead City its name," he replied, sending a chill up my spine. "So hurry up, before I change my mind about helping you."

He quickly moved toward a darkened stairwell that led deeper underground.

"No," I implored him. "We need to go up, not down."

"Considering you've already alerted a least a dozen people that you are, in fact, not undead, the first place they'll look is up. Down is our best shot."

He took to the stairs, and after a brief hesitation I followed him.

"*How* did I alert them that I'm not undead?" I wanted to know as I tried to keep up with him.

"You asked them to identify a picture of a man who everyone in Dead City already knows. The fact that you don't was kind of a big hint."

I was in too much of a panic to wonder why every zombie would know the creep who'd chased my mom and me. "If they knew, why didn't they just attack me there?"

We reached the bottom of the stairs, and he stopped for a moment. He looked at me and shook his head, frustrated by my lack of understanding.

"They're not Level 3s back there," he reminded me. "And 1s and 2s don't *just attack*. They discuss and they coordinate."

"And then?"

"And then . . . if you're lucky, the Level 1s win the

argument and you make it back to the surface with only minor damage. But the 2s . . . they hate to lose."

As I was mulling over this little tidbit, I could hear the roar of water rushing nearby.

"Where are we going?"

"The aqueduct," he informed me as he headed in the next direction. "It's the quickest way out. We can ride the current down to Morningside Park and then go up to the surface there."

"Ride the current?" I asked with disbelief. "You have a boat?"

"No," he laughed. Then he stopped for a moment and looked back at me. "You can swim, can't you?"

That's when I realized that we were going *into* the water.

"Yeah, but laps at the Astoria Park pool are one thing. A raging current in a dark underground tunnel sounds a little dangerous."

"Oh, it's not *a little* dangerous," he said. "It's a lot dangerous. But nothing compared to what happens when an undead mob turns on a breather at a flatline party."

Just the thought of that made me shudder. Then we heard some people following us down the stairs.

"Speaking of which," he said, nodding at the noise. He

pointed toward the darkness. "The aqueduct's this way."

We hurried to a narrow crawl space. He squeezed in and I followed. I was smaller than him, so it was easier for me, but I still began to feel a little claustrophobic.

The sound of the water got louder and louder, until we reached the end of the passageway. Once we came out on the other side we had enough room to stand up, but that was about all. We were on a small ledge directly above the water.

The roar echoed through the tight quarters of the tunnel, and he had to speak up as he gave me instructions. "After you dive in and come back to the surface, try to float on your back, feet first, and keep to the middle. You want to stay as close as possible to the air pocket."

Dive. Surface. Air pocket. Argghhh.

It was all too much. But before I had a chance to think it over, he jumped in and started going down the tunnel. Then I heard voices on the other side of the crawl space getting closer, and I decided I had no choice.

I closed my eyes and then stepped off the ledge.

The water was way colder than I expected, and the pace of the current was really strong. I tried to follow his instructions and float on my back, but I kept slamming into the bricks that formed the ceiling of the aqueduct.

I felt like I was riding one of the slides at the water park we went to last summer at the Jersey shore. Only that was fun and exciting, and there were lifeguards everywhere.

This, on the other hand, was dark and terrifying. And the closest thing I had to a lifeguard was an undead crackpot who was already mad at me for crashing his flatline party.

Before I knew it, I'd lost all track of time and direction. There was a long stretch where the air pocket was only a couple of inches high, making me gag water whenever I tried to breathe.

Then the pace picked up, and I really started zipping along until I shot out of the tube and plunged ten feet through the air before splashing into an underground reservoir. When I bobbed up to the surface, I could hear him calling to me.

"Over here!" he yelled out. "Swim hard!"

It was dark, but I was still able to make him out. He was above the waterline, sitting on some rocks, waving for me to come to him. My instinct was to rest for a moment, but that's when I felt the current trying to pull me down into the reservoir.

"Don't let it pull you under!" he warned. "Just swim to me."

I swam with all the strength I could muster, and finally broke through the current and struggled to the side.

He reached down to help me up, but I was so frantic that I almost ripped his arm out of its socket. (A real possibility with the undead.) Finally, I made it up next to him, collapsing on a rock.

"Are you okay?" he asked me.

I hacked some water and tried to catch my breath. I was finally able to sit up partway by resting back on my elbows. "You know how sometimes you're scared of something, but then you do it and it's so exciting that you end up enjoying it?"

"Yeah," he said, smiling.

I shook my head. "This was nothing like that." I hacked a few more coughs. "That was the single worst experience of my life."

Then I looked at him.

"Thank you."

"You're welcome."

That's when I noticed his left hand. His fingers were broken and bent in different directions, and his wrist had been snapped back at an impossible angle.

"Ooooh. Did I do that when you were helping me out?"

"No," he said with a shrug. "I caught it against the wall right before the plunge."

"Oh yeah . . . *the plunge*!" I shook my head. "There's *no* warning for that one."

He laughed. I just sat there and tried to pull myself together. For about a minute or so we were silent, except for the sound of my heavy breathing and the cracking noise his fingers and wrist made as he snapped them back into place.

Finally I asked, "Where are we?"

"Morningside Park," he answered. "You know it?"

I nodded. "Best place in the city to see great blue herons, red-winged blackbirds, and rock doves," I answered, recalling my days with the Junior Birders. "Especially in the pond by the waterfall."

Morningside Park has an actual waterfall. It's not some phony man-made fountain, but a natural fall that drops about twenty feet into a big pond. It's hard to believe it's in the middle of the city.

"I'll give you this," he said, laughing. "You're not like any breather I've ever met."

"And you're not like any . . . *undead person*"—I caught myself before using the z-word—"I've ever met."

He looked at me for a moment before asking, "What do you want with Marek?"

"Is that his name? The man in the picture?"

He nodded.

"When I was a little girl, he tried to hurt my mother and me," I answered. "I want to know why."

"With Marek, there doesn't have to be a reason *why*. The only thing you need to know about him is that he's a bad guy and someone you want to avoid."

"Let me guess," I joked, in the way you joke about something that terrifies you. "He's one of those Level 2s who hates to lose."

He shook his head and with all seriousness answered, "No, he's the Level 2 who never loses."

"How come?"

"First of all," he said, "he's one of the Unlucky 13."

It was the same thing my mother had written on the envelope with the pictures. "Who are the Unlucky 13?" I asked.

"The very first undead," he replied. "They were miners who were killed in the explosion in 1896 that opened the seam of Manhattan schist."

"Those guys are still around?" I said in disbelief.

He nodded. "And you can build a lot of power in more than a hundred and thirty years of living. They're treated like gods down here. Each one is in charge of a different part of the underground."

"And what's Marek in charge of?" I asked.

He smiled. "He's in charge of the other twelve. He was the foreman on the mining crew, and he's still the boss. They call him the mayor of Dead City."

"I imagine he wouldn't be happy if he found out you helped me."

Liberty shook his head. "No, he would not."

"Then why did you do it?"

He thought about this for a moment before answering. "Omega today. Omega forever."

I couldn't believe it. "You're an Omega?"

He nodded. "And Marek is the one who did this to me," he said as he pointed to the scar that ran along his scalp. "He's determined to get rid of all the Omegas, past and present."

"I don't know how I can thank you," I said.

"First of all, you can get out of here in case any of the others followed us." He pointed toward a walkway. "That takes you right out behind the waterfall."

I stood up and started toward the walkway. Then I stopped and turned back to him. "I know you go by Liberty, but can I ask your real name?"

"Liberty is my real name," he said. "My parents were both American history teachers. What about you?"

"I'm Molly."

"Nice to meet you, Molly," he said, smiling. "Now do me a favor. Stay safe and stay away from Marek . . . no matter what."

I thanked him again and then followed the path until it came out by the waterfall. The passageway was wet, and water poured all over me, but I was too soaked to care.

By the time I made it home, I'd decided to give up my search. Part of this was because Liberty had done such a good job convincing me that it was too dangerous, and part was due to the fact that I had run out of ways to look. Even I wasn't stupid enough to go back into Dead City by myself, and you can't exactly look up "Marek" under "zombies" in the phone book.

But a couple of days later, I was over at Grayson's house using his computer to research a biology paper. Zeus really is an amazing computer. It has access to every database you can imagine, and I like the way it recognizes my voice and calls me by name.

As usual Grayson's brothers, Wyatt and Van, stumbled into the room, arguing about something. I think it had to do with whether or not Pluto should still be considered a planet. He moved the debate out into the family room, and in the process left me alone.

That's when it dawned on me that while I couldn't look up Marek in the phone book, I *could* check for him in the *Book of the Dead*.

Unlike the *Book of Secrets*, Omegas did have limited access to the *Book of the Dead* because we're responsible for taking the census every five years. In fact, the five years were almost up, and Grayson had been working on a new program for the next one.

His theory was that the census usually misses a large portion of the zombie population, and he was trying to come up with a better way of counting them. To test the program, he'd been running data from all the past censuses through Zeus.

I accessed the program and then ran a search for the name Marek. Zeus instantly spit out four different entries. Each was from a different year and each Marek had a different last name. The most recent was Marek Fulton in 1975. It seemed like a dead end, but then something about the last names caught my attention. They were Bedford, Linden, Nostrand, and Fulton.

They sounded familiar and I realized why. Each one was also the name of a major road in Brooklyn. They had to be fake surnames used by one person named Marek, trying to hide his identity.

I could hear Grayson and his brothers still arguing and figured I had a few minutes. I ran a search for all the names of streets in Brooklyn, and then cross-referenced them with the name Marek.

I've got to say, Zeus is some kind of powerful, because in about ten seconds a single name was flashing on the screen:

MAREK DRIGGS, CONSULTANT,

NYC SANDHOGS LOCAL 147

There was also a phone number listed.

Normally, I would never have thought of calling because of caller ID. But I had Zeus at my fingertips, and Grayson had set him up with a program that blocked it.

I knew Grayson was going to be back any second, so it was now or never.

I had Zeus dial the number.

Just when I was about to hang up, I heard a click on the other end, then a man's voice.

"Hello?"

I Create a Fake Identity

Until now, he had simply been an anonymous face in a recurring nightmare. The face of the man who had chased my mother and me. The man who had terrified me and created my paralyzing fear of heights. But now that face had a name . . . and a voice.

"Hello?" he repeated.

The voice wasn't ominous like I'd expected, but was actually kind of friendly instead. Still, I gulped before answering.

"Is this Marek Driggs? With the Sandhogs?"

"Yes, it is. Can I help you?"

I may not always be a quick thinker, but I was sitting in front of a computer that more than made up for it. After just a few mouse clicks, Zeus was spitting out page after page of information about Marek Driggs and the Sandhogs Local 147. As the pages filled the trio of monitors in front of me, I came up with a plan.

"I'm working on a project for school," I said, trying not to stammer. "About the Sandhogs."

The Sandhogs are the urban miners who dig the tunnels beneath Manhattan, and Local 147 is the labor union that represents them. The pictures scrolling across Zeus's monitors told their amazing story. At any given moment hundreds of workers are operating giant earth-moving equipment and tunneling machinery underneath one of the busiest cities in the world. And hardly anybody even knows they exist.

"That's fantastic," he said, sounding like he truly meant it. "It's about time the local schools paid some attention to the Sandhogs. You know, without them this city wouldn't be possible."

"They're the men who make New York work," I said, reading their slogan from the website in front of me.

"That's exactly right!"

"That's what I want to write about," I told him, gaining

confidence. "And for the assignment we're supposed to do an interview."

"Well, I'm not with the press office," he replied. "But I don't know anybody who understands the underground quite like I do."

"Well, then," I said, "maybe I could interview you."

And that's how I ended up making an appointment to interview Marek Driggs in his office.

I knew this went against everything Dr. H and Liberty had told me. But for reasons I didn't fully understand, I *needed* to see him face-to-face. Both for me and for my mom. And unlike the flatline party, where I was ill prepared and made stupid mistakes, this time I had a good idea of what I was doing and who I was up against. I was going to be careful and smart.

I spent the next few days learning everything I could about the Sandhogs. The more I read, the more I was amazed by what they do. The Sandhogs are constantly at work underneath the city. And their history made them the perfect hiding place for the undead. The original zombies and some of the earliest Sandhogs both came from the crew of miners who dug the city's first subway tunnel. And what better place is there for a zombie to work than deep beneath the city, surrounded by Manhattan schist?

I wasn't planning to confront Marek. I just wanted to study him and figure out why he and my mother were enemies.

I had one big advantage. He still looked like he did when I first saw him, but I had aged and looked nothing like my five-year-old self.

That Thursday I was totally confident when I left school and went to the union headquarters. It's located in Washington Heights, in the shadow of the George Washington Bridge. Before I went in, I put my Omega training to good use. I walked around the building look-ing for possible escape routes, just in case something did go wrong. And in my head I ran through my phony identity one more time to make sure I had it down. Unlike with Liberty, I was not about to give this guy my real name.

By the time I walked up to the receptionist, I was com-pletely prepared.

"Hello. My name is Jennifer Steinbach, and I'm a stu-dent at Bronx Science," I told her, using the name and school of the girl who'd beaten me at last year's regional science fair. "I'm supposed to interview Mr. Driggs for a research paper I'm writing."

So far, so good.

"Yes," she said with a smile. "You're a few minutes

early. So why don't you sit down with the others?"

It took a moment for what she said to register. "Others?"

She motioned to a nearby waiting area, where I saw the very unhappy trio of Natalie, Alex, and Grayson. I didn't want to let the receptionist see my surprise, so I gave them a smile and a little wave.

"Hey, guys."

Not one of them smiled back. They just glowered as I walked over to join them.

"What are you doing here?" I asked under my breath as I sat next to Natalie.

"Well, considering you couldn't come up with anything better than Jennifer Steinbach and a research paper," she answered, "I'd say we're saving you."

"How'd you even know I was going to be here?"

She nodded toward Grayson. "He told us."

I looked at Grayson. "Who told you?"

He couldn't help but smirk ever so slightly. "Zeus."

I couldn't believe it.

"A computer . . . *tattled* on me?"

"No, but it did generate a report on your unexpected search into the *Book of the Dead*. And the voice recognition software recorded your phone call because it detected a high level of distress in your speech patterns."

"You shouldn't be here," I whispered to them. "This has nothing to do with you. Besides, I can handle it by myself."

"If that's what you think," Alex said, looking right into my eyes, "then you haven't listened to a thing we've tried to teach you. *Omega today, Omega forever.* You can't turn it off and on. We're a team. And by the way, you can't handle it by yourself."

Before I could respond, a well-dressed man in a suit came out to greet us. He had a boyish face with rosy cheeks, and was definitely not Marek Driggs.

"Are you the students for the interview?" he asked with a friendly smile, no hint of New York in his accent.

I stood up to greet him. "Yes, but I thought we were meeting with Mr. Driggs."

"You are," he answered. "I'm his assistant, Michael. I'm just here to take you to his office."

At first I thought it was kind of strange because the headquarters weren't particularly big. It didn't seem like we'd need a guide. But then Michael opened a cabinet and started pulling out red hard hats with the Sandhogs logo on the side.

"What are those for?" Alex asked.

"Didn't you know?" Michael responded. "Mr. Driggs

keeps his office underground, close to the construction site. He always wants to be near the workers, so that he can best address their needs and concerns."

The four of us shared a desperate look, and I was ready to call off the whole thing when Natalie stepped to the front.

"Sounds cool," she said, totally selling it. "How do we get underground?"

Without realizing it, I had put my friends into the impossible situation I most wanted to avoid. In order to help me, they were going to have to break rules they did not want to break. They were about to head into Dead City, and there was no way to alert the Prime-O.

Michael led us out of the building and down the street for a couple of blocks until we reached a construction site. He went to talk to a security guard, which left us alone for a moment.

"I am so sorry," I told them. "I didn't want to drag you into this."

"Well, we're dragged," Natalie said. "So we might as well do this right." She paused for a moment. "We'll deal with how angry we are later."

"What can you tell us about Driggs?" Alex asked.

"He's very secretive and very bad," I told them. "He's

one of the original thirteen zombies dating back to the subway explosion in 1896. And he's the guy who chased my mom and me when I was a kid. The time when we got stuck out on the roof."

"Really?" Grayson was concerned. He knew how much that moment haunted me. "You're certain it's him?"

I nodded.

"Well, that explains why you went crazy," Alex said with a laugh that actually made me feel better. "But I'll tell you, there's one thing I'll never be able to forgive you for."

"What's that?"

"Making us from Bronx Science. They're our biggest rivals. You know how much I hate those guys."

He smiled and winked, and I realized how lucky I was to have the three of them as friends.

Michael came back from the guard shack. "We're all set," he said. "Just make sure you keep on your hard hats the entire time."

He led us to a large freight elevator. Instead of a door, it had a gate that Michael had to pull down until it snapped closed. As the elevator descended, we could look through the links of the gate and see the different layers of rock as we passed them.

"We're going down about thirty floors," Michael said,

his voice rising so he could be heard over the elevator's motor. "But there's only one stop, so it doesn't take long."

When the elevator reached the bottom, we stepped out into a world unlike anything I'd ever seen. We were in a massive cavern at least a hundred feet high. I couldn't even see the ceiling because all the dust from the digging formed a haze above our heads. We practically had to yell to be heard over the rock pulverizers.

"It looks like something out of a science-fiction movie," Grayson said.

I nodded. "Exactly what I was thinking."

"Let's hope it's not one of the science-fiction movies where the aliens eat the arriving astronauts," Alex joked, leaning in.

I looked up and saw a line of giant dump trucks belching exhaust as they climbed through tunnels that spiderwebbed in every direction. For the life of me I couldn't figure out how they got all the equipment down here. Michael must have read my mind because he explained it to us.

"A lot of the time, they have to take the equipment apart on the surface, send it down in the elevator in pieces, and rebuild it here. It's amazing, isn't it?"

"Yes, it is," Natalie said, truly impressed.

"Marek's office is right over here," he said as he led us to a trailer on the edge of the construction site.

Seeing a photo of Marek Driggs was one thing. I didn't realize how hard it would be to see him face-to-face. I almost screamed when he met us at the door.

When we locked eyes, I had no doubt he was the man who had chased my mother and me. But I couldn't believe how much he had cleaned himself up. Even down here in an underground construction trailer, he was dressed in a suit like a Wall Street lawyer.

It didn't help that he was incredibly charming and friendly. He greeted each one of us with a big smile and a hearty handshake. He even offered us sodas from his mini-fridge.

"How was the ride down?" he asked us. "Something, isn't it?"

"Yes, sir," Natalie said, taking charge when it was apparent I was too tongue-tied.

"Well, I can't tell you how pleased I am that you all have shown an interest in what we do down here." He turned to his assistant. "Michael, give us thirty minutes. Then they'll need an escort back."

I was frightened simply seeing him, but the really terrifying thing was how nice he was. If I didn't know what

I knew, I would have been totally fooled. He told us about the history of the Sandhogs and some of the important projects they had completed. He pulled out diagrams and blueprints and explained how the tunneling worked and what they did with all the rock they dug out.

He gave us everything we'd need to write a thorough term paper and absolutely nothing that helped me understand why he tormented my mother or why Liberty said he was so dangerous.

I hated to say it, but he seemed awesome.

Then, when there were about five minutes left, he looked right at me.

"You know," he said, "even in the bad light we have down here, you have absolutely beautiful eyes."

It was awkward, and I didn't know how to respond.

"Thank you."

Then he dropped the bomb.

"You look so much like your mother."

The Mayor of Dead City

All the color drained from my face.

Marek laughed and flashed a wicked smile before saying, "Well, now who looks like a zombie?"

I couldn't believe he had recognized me. I couldn't believe I had put myself and my friends into this much danger. We were three hundred feet deep in Dead City, alone with the most evil Level 2 zombie of all.

And nobody knew we were here.

"You know, you really do look like your mother," he continued. "And I'll tell you, she would have been proud of you for figuring out who I was and finding me so quickly. The apple doesn't fall far.

"But she would have been disappointed in this: you coming here so unprepared, putting your friends and yourself in danger. She would have been very disappointed."

I started to tremble as I thought about the words that Liberty had used: *"He's determined to get rid of all the Omegas, past and present."*

"Don't listen to him, Molly," Alex said, jumping in. "He's not going to do anything to any of us."

Marek turned to him. "Is that so? What makes you think that?"

"Too many people know we're down here," he said, bluffing. "Our teacher, the Prime-O, the receptionist, your assistant. Besides, we had an appointment. It's marked in your official calendar. Even if you tried to erase it, a computer tech from the police department would find it in less than two minutes. You can't risk those types of loose ends."

Marek nodded, savoring the moment. "First of all, there's no way you told your teacher or the Prime-O; they wouldn't have let you come. As to the receptionist and the assistant, they're both undead, so I'm pretty sure my secrets are safe with them. You are right about the appointment. That would be a problem, except that the appointment was for Jennifer Steinbach of Bronx Science. Lovely girl and *very* much alive. In fact, we had her over earlier today, so the Sandhogs could present her with a plaque in honor of her win at last year's science fair. I even posed for a picture with her, you know, to tie up any loose ends."

Alex slumped. His bluff had been called.

"As far as the rest of the world is concerned, you four might as well be on Mars," Marek said as he turned to me. "You know, it's funny—if only you'd been honest when you made the appointment. You would have saved everyone."

What happened next was unexpected. Grayson stood up and looked at Marek defiantly. "And if you had been honest, it might have saved you."

"What are you talking about?" he asked.

"Just some other loose ends that you've overlooked."

"Really?" Marek said. "We're going to go through this with each one of you? Okay, I'll play along. How many loose ends did I forget this time?"

"One thousand seven hundred and eighteen."

Marek laughed. "That's a specific number. Tell me, what is it?"

"It's the number of Sandhogs Local 147 members who

will get e-mails from me tonight if I don't cancel the send command by seven o'clock."

For the first time since we'd arrived, Marek was momentarily speechless as he tried to read Grayson, to see whether he was bluffing too.

"And what do these *alleged* e-mails say?"

"They detail the tens of thousands of dollars you have stolen from the hardworking members of this union over the years. Money that you've deposited into private accounts to spend on whatever it is that freak-show zombies like you do for fun."

It was the first time I'd ever heard Grayson use the z-word. And I have to say it was well-timed, because Marek froze in his tracks.

"What can I say?" Grayson added, with total badass confidence. "I was bored this weekend, and I have a *really* good computer."

Natalie jumped into the fun. "After they arrest you, what do you think the odds are that they'll send you to a prison constructed out of Manhattan schist?" She made a choking sound, imitating what Marek's final breaths would be like.

He considered this for a moment, looked at Grayson, and cocked his head. "Perhaps I underestimated you," he said. "Although I suppose I wouldn't be the first to do that."

"And you won't be the last," Grayson responded, not backing down one bit. "Because my friends and I are going to walk out of here completely unharmed."

Marek nodded and actually looked impressed by what Grayson had done. "That leaves us at something of an impasse. Maybe we should try that memory device you Omegas use in these confrontations? What is it called, CLAP?"

He knew a lot more about the Omegas than I would have liked.

"*C* is for 'calm,' right?"

No one responded.

"I'll take your silence as a yes. Well, we're being calm, so that's a good start. *L* is for 'listen.' So listen to this: Even if you did send those e-mails, I can disappear underground for longer than you can imagine. It may delay my plans a little, but I will come back and I will win. So all you've done is buy yourself time. Don't push your luck.

"As to *A* and 'avoidance,' trust me when I say you want to avoid me from now on. We've had our fun, but it's over and I've got work to do. Which leaves us with *P*, the reason you want to avoid me. Because if you don't, I will punish you in far worse ways than any you've thought of. I won't just hurt you. I will take from you the things you hold dear. Just as they were taken from me."

He leaned close to Alex and whispered in his ear.

"For example, those little sisters you love so much. It would be awful if something happened to them."

Alex shoved him and looked ready to fight on the spot. But Natalie put a calming hand on his shoulder, and he managed to control himself.

"I'm not saying that I'm going to hurt them," Marek continued. "I just want you to understand that the best thing about being a Level 2 is the fact that having no soul means having no conscience. I can do something you find completely reprehensible and not lose a second of sleep over it."

He turned to me and gave me his most evil look yet. "You know, I slept like a baby the night I killed your mother."

I went to instant boil, which is exactly what he wanted. "Don't even try that with me," I snapped. "You had nothing to do with her death. My mother died of cancer."

Marek nodded. "Yes, she did. She died of a very specific type of cancer that occurs when dead human tissue penetrates an open wound and passes along its own sickness and disease to the living. Most people, like your father, think that happened by accident while she was performing an autopsy. But would you like to know where the flesh really came from?"

He slipped off his jacket and unbuttoned his shirt cuff at his left wrist. He slowly rolled up his sleeve to reveal that his arm was covered with hideous scars and gashes. Chunks of rotted flesh clung to exposed bone.

I almost threw up looking at it.

"This is why you came here, isn't it, Molly?" he asked, holding the arm up for me to see. "You wanted to find out something about me. Well, you've succeeded. I am a grotesque monster."

He rolled the sleeve back down and then buttoned it just as his assistant returned to escort us back.

"Perfect timing, Michael," Marek said happily. "We just finished. I think we've all learned some valuable lessons. Don't you?"

None of us felt the need to continue the charade by answering.

"I'll take your silence as a yes," he said, undeterred. "Good luck on your term paper. You should have a lot to write about."

The five of us remained quiet during the entire elevator ride to the surface. I was in a daze, wondering if it was at all possible that Marek had actually caused my mother's death. Even more important, I was worried I had endangered my friends and their families.

Natalie was to my right. She put a comforting arm across my shoulder and gave it a reassuring squeeze.

"It's going to be okay," she whispered. "He was just trying to scare us."

"It worked."

I looked over at Michael and realized that the rosy complexion I had noticed on his cheeks was, in fact, makeup. Marek had told the truth about him. He was undead.

Once we turned in our hard hats and left the work site, Natalie moved to the curb and signaled for a cab.

"Let's give it up for Grayson," Alex said, offering him a high five. "Hero of the day."

"Absolutely," I added with a grin. "I can't believe you were able to break into his banking records."

"About that . . . ," Grayson said. I noticed his hand was trembling.

"What's the matter?" I asked.

"That was all a bluff," he said with a gulp.

"No way," Alex said, even more impressed. "You *are* the man."

"How did you know he'd stolen money from the Sand-hogs?" I asked.

Grayson was still a little shaken. "He's a bad guy with no conscience. I figured he had to have stolen something. Money seemed like the most logical guess."

I shook my head in disbelief. "You guys are something else."

A cab pulled over and we all got in. It was a minivan. Alex and Grayson took the rear seat while Natalie and I got in the middle row.

"Where to?" the driver asked.

"To 520 First Avenue," Natalie said. "The Office of Chief Medical Examiner."

"We're going to the morgue?" I asked.

Natalie shook her head. "No. We're going to see the Prime-O."

Consequences

Like me, Natalie was convinced that, in addition to being New York's best medical examiner, Dr. H was also the Prime Omega. And after what we'd just been through, she knew we needed to go straight to the top. She called him from the cab and said we were coming in.

The final proof he was who we suspected: He didn't try to stop us.

We walked into the building, and if ever I could have used one of Jamaican Bob's corny jokes to break the tension, this was the time. But he must have sensed something serious was going on. Instead of a joke, all we got was a faint smile as he told us, "Dr. Hidalgo is expecting you."

The closest I got to a laugh was right before we walked into the lab. Natalie and I each swiped some vanilla under our noses and offered it to the boys. They looked at us like we were aliens.

"I think we'll be fine," Alex assured us.

"Yeah," Grayson added smugly. "It's not the first time we've ever been in a lab."

It was, however, the first time they'd ever been in the morgue. Within thirty seconds, they were begging for some extract. Natalie and I shared a smile.

It was the last time she smiled at me for quite a while.

More than anywhere else, the key moments of my life occurred within the walls of the lab at the New York City morgue. This is where my mother and I created a bond that made the rest of my family call me Mini-Mom. And when her death turned my world upside down, this was where I started to rebuild my soul. More recently, it was where Natalie and I formed the first true friendship of my life. And even more recently than that, it was where I came into my own as an Omega in a battle with three killer zombies.

Amazingly, in a room everyone else associates with death, my memories of the morgue were everything but. They were all vibrant and very much alive.

Until now.

That's because "dead" is the only word to describe the expression on Dr. Hidalgo's face as Natalie detailed what had happened between us and Marek Driggs. She recounted the entire chain of events, and the revelation about my mother's death and the threats he made against us and our families.

When she was done, I told him the story of my solo visit to Dead City. About how I crashed the flatline party and escaped with Liberty in the aqueduct. I even admitted that I had visited the Alpha Bakery without any imminent need.

I didn't want any more secrets. By the time I was done, I couldn't look any of them in the eye.

"Well," Dr. H said, digesting the weight of what we'd just shared. "I am so relieved you all are safe. And I appreciate the honesty in what you've told me."

He hesitated for a moment.

"You have told me *everything*, haven't you?"

All eyes turned to me.

"Yes, sir," I said, barely able to get it out.

As the Prime-O, Dr. H held all the power. He didn't need to confer or consult with anyone. He didn't even need time to mull it over. He was judge and jury, and wasted no time before giving us his verdict.

"First, for the three of you," he said to the others. "You broke one of our most important rules by going into Dead City without notifying me. The primary purpose of this rule is to keep you from winding up in a dangerous situation exactly like the one you found yourselves in. You should all know better. You did it to protect your teammate in very unusual circumstances, and while that counts for something, there must be consequences."

Alex flinched.

"This team will be inactive until further notice, while we determine the extent of your exposure and danger," Dr. H continued. "I hope you will use this time to consider the seriousness of what you've done. You are not to engage in *any* activities as an Omega Team . . . with one exception."

The "exception" caught Natalie by surprise. "What's that?" she asked.

Dr. Hidalgo took a quick breath, looked at me, and then back at her. "You can get together at the school or at Grayson's house in Brooklyn to discuss candidates to replace Molly."

The word hit me in the gut worse than any punch from a zombie ever could.

"Replace?" I asked weakly.

Dr. H turned to me, and I saw a tear running down his cheek. The only other time I had seen him cry was at my mother's funeral. I knew this was killing him.

"Molly, you're family to me," he said, shaking his head. "But you've shown such bad judgment. You've risked your life and the lives of your teammates. You simply cannot be an Omega. At least, not now. Maybe next year or the year after that. If I think you're ready, I'll let the teams looking for new members know. But until then, you're out."

I was devastated. But I knew he was right. I had to take responsibility for what I'd done.

"Do you understand the consequences of your actions?"

I tried to speak, but all I could do was nod.

Much to my surprise, another voice spoke out for me.

"I'm sorry, but I find that unacceptable."

It was Natalie.

My surprise was nothing compared to Dr. Hidalgo's. He was downright angry.

"I beg your pardon?"

"With all due respect, I find your decision unacceptable." Her voice was cracking a little, but she didn't back down. "I know you have been very close to Molly and her family for a long time. I think the emotions of that connection might be affecting your decision."

Dr. H gritted his teeth and tried to maintain his composure.

"I assure you that they are not," he said.

"Even so, as the captain of this team, I believe I have the right to appeal any ruling to a review board of past Omegas. And that is what I would like to do."

I actually remembered this from one of my training sessions with Grayson. But he had made it sound like it was a technicality, not something that ever happened.

"Do you dispute any of what you and Molly have told me here?" Dr. Hidalgo asked her.

"No," she said.

"Then what do you plan on telling the review board that you think will make a difference?"

I can guarantee you that no friend in my entire life will ever stand up for me as much as Natalie did at this very moment.

"First of all," she began, "I will tell them that Molly is the sole reason why the *Book of Secrets* is not in the hands of the undead. That if it were not for her quick thinking and fast action, the lives of *every* Omega, past and present, would be in danger."

I looked over to her, but she avoided eye contact with me. She kept a laser focus on Dr. H.

"I will tell them that the reason she was able to do this is because she is the most naturally gifted Omega that any of the three of us has ever seen. And that because of this natural ability, she completed her training in record time. I should have realized this speed cut into important lessons that would have better prepared her judgment and adherence to the rules. I didn't realize that she wasn't ready, and as her leader, I should have."

I watched Dr. Hidalgo as his face turned from angry to something else harder to define. He wasn't agreeing with her, but he was listening.

"Most important, I will tell them that up until now, this Omega Team has had an impeccable record and a one-hundred-percent success rate. I feel confident in saying that by any standard, this team is elite. And we have absolutely no interest in finding a replacement. Molly's our fourth. There's no one else we'd want."

"Don't you think you should talk to your other teammates before you make such a claim?" he asked her.

Natalie didn't even glance at Alex or Grayson. "I don't need to. I know what they'd say."

Even if she wasn't going to, Dr. Hidalgo looked to the two of them. They nodded their agreement without hesitation. All three were putting their reputations behind me. I didn't deserve it, but I was beyond grateful.

The room fell silent in the way that only the morgue can be as Dr. Hidalgo thought about this. Once he'd considered it, he looked at her.

"Okay," he said, nodding. "You're correct. You do have the right to appeal my decision to the review board. I will tell you that no panel has *ever* overridden the ruling of the Prime-O. And I see no reason why they'd do it this time. But you obviously feel passionate about this, and I respect that."

I smiled and turned to Natalie, but she still wouldn't make eye contact with me. She was mad, and she had every right to be.

"I will pass along your request," he said, "once my successor has been chosen."

"Your successor?" Natalie asked.

"The identity of the Prime-O must be a secret," he explained. "That is no longer the case. My last order will be to put eyes on you and your families. And more important, I will put them on Marek."

"That's going to be hard," I said. "I don't think he comes up to the surface much."

He flashed a tight-lipped smile. "Molly, you're not the only Omega with natural gifts."

"I'm sorry, Dr. H. I didn't mean anything—"

He silenced me with an upturned hand. Then he addressed us all.

"Until further notice, this Omega Team is dissolved."

23

You're Probably (Still) Wondering Why There's a Dead Body in the Bathroom

Despite their strong support in front of Dr. H, the others didn't exactly welcome me with open arms once we'd left the morgue. I couldn't blame them for being mad. I'd done a lot of things wrong. But the worst may well have been that I did them by myself. I forgot that no matter what, I was part of a team.

For the next few days, I gave them plenty of space at school. I avoided the cafeteria and ate my lunch out on the patio overlooking the river.

They came around. Slowly.

Grayson was the first. By Thursday, he had migrated out to the patio too. He wasn't very chatty, but we sat together and watched the boats traveling along the river. Sometimes he'd forget he was mad at me and would make a joke or tell me some odd piece of trivia.

Alex came next. I was sitting in the library one day when he sat down across the table from me.

"Just tell me one thing," he demanded, a stern look on his face.

I braced for the worst and asked, "What?"

"What's it like to ride in the aqueduct?" He flashed a smile. "I've always wanted to do that."

"It's terrifying," I said with a relieved laugh. "Absolutely terrifying."

"But still fun, right?"

"No! It's not fun at all."

"Really? 'Cause it seems like it would be."

A few days later, I was leaving campus after school and I saw that Natalie was right in front of me. I realized that I was going to have to take the first step toward making things better, so I caught up with her.

"I know I said I was sorry," I started, not waiting for any sort of acknowledgment. "But I also should have said thank you."

"Why?" she asked, still not looking at me. "For challenging Dr. H and forcing a review board? For getting my team dissolved?"

"No," I answered. "For being my friend."

She turned her head ever so slightly, the closest I'd come to any sort of opening.

"I've never had a friend before," I continued, "at least not one that I'd count. And as much as I love being an Omega, and I really love it, it's nothing compared to how much it means to be your friend."

"You've got a funny way of showing it." Her tone was short, but I detected the faintest hint of kindness in her expression. An ever so slight thaw.

"I know. I'm terrible at it. Like I said, this is all new to me. You gave me Omega training, but you should have given me *friend* training. I could have used lessons like: 'Five Ways to Show a Friend You Care' or 'Things You're Not Supposed to Do in a Friendship.'"

"I'll tell you the first one," she answered. "You're not supposed to lie. Ever. And you're not supposed to go behind your friend's back."

She was being honest. But she was also beginning to warm up a bit.

"What about endangering your friends' lives?"

"No," she said, laughing. "You definitely should not endanger your friends' lives."

"You see, now I'm getting it. This is exactly the type of training I needed."

We kept talking until we reached the tram. She swiped her transit card and walked through the turnstile. I was just about to do the same when she turned back to me.

"What are you doing?"

"Swiping my card."

"For the tram?" she said, in total disbelief. "You're terrified of the tram."

"Completely."

Finally, she looked me in the eye and smiled.

"You would ride this tram? The tram that dangles more than two hundred and fifty feet in the air?" she asked, taunting. "Just to show me how much you want to be my friend?"

"I might scream and pass out along the way, but yes, I would."

She reached out to stop me from swiping my card.

"You don't have to," she answered, to my great relief. "I'll see you tomorrow."

That was earlier this week, which brings me to the St. Andrew's Prep fencing tournament where this story began.

If you remember (and I tend to ramble, so I know it's hard to keep up), when I started to tell you about all of this, I was sitting in a bathroom stall with a dead body. That's where I still am. Trapped and waiting for help to arrive.

It is definitely not the way I expected this Saturday to unfold. As an alternate, my job was supposed to be keeping score for my coach. I was also hoping to get a feel for the strategies used by some of the girls from different schools, because I really want to get good at this.

I didn't find out I was going to compete until a few minutes before the first bout. (In fencing, the individual matches are called "bouts.") Coach Wilkes had to turn in our official lineup, and Hannah Gilbert still hadn't shown up. When he couldn't reach her on her cell, he gave me her spot on the team.

The fact that I hadn't had any time to worry about competing in an actual tournament was probably a good thing. There were no expectations and no pressure. Any points I could earn for my team were a bonus.

In my first bout, I fell behind quickly, only to suddenly go on a roll. In an odd way, all the anger, rage, and frustration I had from recent events found their way into my fencing. I didn't give up a single point in the next two bouts, and before I knew it, I was in the finals.

I was up against Saige Simpson, the top-ranked girl fencer in metropolitan New York. She had already accepted a scholarship to fence at Notre Dame and hadn't lost a single bout all season. Everyone assumed she was going to kill me. But I knew better. I looked at her and came to an instant conclusion.

She didn't have a chance.

That's because the way she wins is through intimidation. Every other girl in the city was scared to face her, and that gave her an unbelievable advantage. But I wasn't scared. I'd faced Level 3 killers, survived a twenty-block ride in an underground river, ripped an undead man's arm out of its socket. I mean, the list goes on and on. To me, Saige Simpson is just another girl.

When I won, I don't know who was more surprised— Saige or my coach. Both had tears in their eyes. My team loved it, and pretty soon they were all pouring bottles of Gatorade on my head, which is why I had to take a shower.

I had just finished showering when the zombie arrived. It was Cornelius Blackwell, still mad about me chopping off his hand. I know I wasn't supposed to participate in Omega activities, but I didn't really have a choice. I had to get rid of him. When I was done, I dragged him into the toilet stall and then texted Natalie, Alex, and Grayson for help.

So now you're caught up. When we started I warned you that you wouldn't believe it, but it's all true.

Also true, I wish I had my vanilla because Cornelius's rapidly decomposing corpse really stinks. I don't know how long I've been here, but I'm going stir crazy.

Finally, I hear someone come into the locker room.

"Molly," a voice calls out in a whisper. "Are you here?"

"Back here," I reply. "The handicapped stall at the end."

I get up, slide the latch, and begin opening the door.

"Are you alone?" the voice continues.

I go to answer as I step out into the bathroom. But then I see him and my heart begins to race. I don't know how it's happened, but I am looking right into the cold dead eyes of Marek Driggs.

I try to move my lips but nothing comes out.

"I'll take your silence as a yes."

Reckoning

I stand there, staring at Marek and desperately trying to devise a plan.

"Am I too late for the tournament?" he asks. "I read about it on your team's website and so wanted to watch you compete. Even though you were only an alternate, I had a *feeling* you'd get a chance."

Suddenly it dawns on me that he may have had something to do with Hannah Gilbert not showing up. He reads the panic in my eyes.

"Don't worry," he assures me. "An unfortunate accident, but the fracture was clean, and she should heal nicely."

Marek Driggs is pure evil.

"What did *she* ever do to you?"

"Ab-so-lute-ly noth-ing," he says, drawing out each syllable. "But don't you remember the part about my not having a soul? I needed to get you into the tournament so that you'd be nice and tired by the time we had this little chat. Still, I had no idea you would win. You are a girl of many talents. Hopefully, *reasoning* is one of them."

"We're not in Dead City," I remind him. "There are laws up here on the surface. Trust me when I say you do not want to be caught in a girls' locker room. All I need to do is scream."

"True," he replies, with a thoughtful nod of his head. "But I don't think you want to be caught with a dead body." He motions to Cornelius Blackwell's corpse in the toilet stall. "So let's just keep this between you and me."

It occurs to me that Cornelius was also part of the plan. "Did you send him to tire me out too?"

Marek nods. "Guilty. And I even knew you'd kill him. Truly a terrible thing to do to your own brother. If I had a . . . you know . . . I'd feel awful about it."

I glance at the floor and see my fencing gear. I realize that if I can stall him just a little as I move toward it, I might be able to grab a weapon.

"Cornelius was your brother?" I ask, buying myself time.

"Yes. In fact, there were five Blackwell brothers in that subway explosion. Five among the Unlucky 13 banished to spend eternity half alive and half dead on this wretched island. And I'll let you in on a little secret."

He leans forward and whispers, "One of my brothers . . . is someone you know. Betcha can't guess who."

Marek flashes a wicked grin, and for the first time, I can see that his back teeth have a little orange and yellow to them.

"I seriously doubt that," I say as I take another tiny side step. "I don't really hang out with *your* kind."

He mulls that over for a second.

"I'll make a deal with you. I'll tell you who my brother is. And then I'll spread the word among . . . *my* kind . . . that you are not to be touched. Believe me, if that's what I say, no one will so much as lay a finger on you. Ever."

"And what do you want from me in return?"

"The *Book of Secrets*," he says, his eyes burning orange with sudden rage. "Cornelius said you took it from him, and I want it back."

I shift my weight, as though I'm considering this, and use that movement to cover another mini-step toward the gear. I'm almost close enough.

"Why do you want it?"

"Why do I want a book that will lead me to the identity of every Omega past and present?" he asks sarcastically. "Let's just say I'm planning on throwing a party, and I want to make sure everybody's invited."

"I've got bad news," I tell him. "I don't have it anymore."

"Pity." The smile disappears from his face. "I guess that means I have no use for you."

It's now or never.

I make my move toward the bag. But it's not a real move. It's an *appel*—the fake out I learned in fencing. Rather than reach for the bag, I move in that direction and stomp my foot.

Marek, who has had his eye on the bag the whole time, jumps to cut me off, and in the process winds up completely out of position.

I use one of my favorite Jeet Kune Do moves to introduce my foot to the back of his skull. Before he knows what's hit him, I follow with two quick punches, all the while reminding myself what Alex taught me that first day: *Go for the head. Go for the head.*

He grabs a weapon from my bag and then flails wildly at me. I dodge the blade and grab one of my own.

Real sword fights aren't like you imagine them. And they certainly aren't like you see in the movies. They're quick and messy and confusing. There's no time to think or plan and certainly no time for clever lines.

And while training had made me a better sword fighter than him, he has an advantage that I cannot overcome. I discover it as I make a great move to run my sword right into his gut, only to have the blade make a clanking sound and bend back at me.

I stare at it in confusion as he laughs.

"Oops," he says with delight. "Is this against the rules?"

He raps his chest and there's a loud *thwack*. Then he undoes a button to reveal a layer of body armor.

"It's the kind of thing that . . . how did your friend put it? Oh yeah . . . that freak-show zombies like me buy with our money."

I decide my best strategy is to stop fighting and to escape. Long rows of lockers fill the room, and I duck behind one to try to play hide-and-seek with Marek.

I think back to how Liberty rescued me at the flatline party. He took me deeper when everyone thought I'd go straight for the surface. I use the same logic on Marek. Rather than head for the door, where he expects, I go for the window.

By the time he figures out what's happened, I've already

climbed down to the sidewalk and have a block-and-a-half head start.

As much as I hate heights, I look desperately for a skyscraper to get away from him. But there aren't any in this part of town. It turns out skyscrapers are just like cabs. There's never one around when you need it.

My only hope is to get off the island. That's when I see my salvation: Looming high above me, just a few blocks away, is the George Washington Bridge.

If you've never seen it, the GWB is amazing. It's a suspension bridge that crosses the Hudson River into New Jersey. It's held up by two massive towers made entirely of exposed steel beams.

Not until I am running along the walkway, however, do I realize how impressive it is. The bridge is nearly a *mile* long, and a full day of fencing and zombie fighting is beginning to catch up with me.

As I reach the first tower, I look over my shoulder and see Marek gaining on me. I don't know where the magic line is that he cannot cross without losing the power from the Manhattan schist, but he's still picking up speed and I'm slowing down big-time.

That's when I make a drastic decision.

At the base of the tower I see a maintenance elevator.

Actually, calling it an elevator is a stretch. Technically, it's a cage with a motor and a gear that climbs up a row of teeth leading all the way to the top. I climb in, slam the cage shut, and press the button for up. The motor whines to life, and the gear slowly begins to turn.

Just as the cage starts to climb, Marek grabs on to the bottom. The engine squeals and strains and then begins to pull him up into the air. I stomp on his fingers as they reach through the links and hear a couple of them snap. Finally, he lets go and I start my climb to the top of the tower.

As I go higher and higher, I try my best not to hyperventilate. We studied the GWB in a class about how suspension bridges work, and I learned the towers are sixty-five stories high . . . a fact I now wish I had forgotten.

When I finally reach the top, I step out into a room where all the suspension cables rest. The science geek in me is amazed by these mammoth steel ropes and the fact that they are able to hold so much. The rest of me is just terrified.

The only thing motivating me is that I am certain Marek won't risk coming this high. I'm more than six hundred and fifty feet away from the nearest Manhattan schist. I can wait here until I'm rescued by workers or find a way to call for help.

Just as I start to catch my breath, I hear the engine of the elevator come back to life.

I don't know how, but Marek is coming.

I figure it will take the elevator five minutes to go all the way down and back up again. That gives me five minutes to figure out a plan.

I step out from the room and onto the top of the tower and cannot believe my eyes. There's no railing or protection of any kind. Just a knee-high edge and a sixty-five-story drop in every direction.

I am frozen with fear.

A strong wind howls around me, and I worry it will knock me over. I gasp and fall to my hands and knees, trying to catch my breath. Even if I wasn't scared of heights, this would be terrifying. As it is, it might be more than I can handle.

I hear the elevator returning, and the only plan I can come up with is to wait by the door and hit Marek with everything I've got the second he steps through it. If I can knock him down and get back to the elevator first, I can escape.

Instead of walking, I crawl into position so that I don't have to look over the edge.

When he steps through the doorway, I summon every

ounce of strength I have left and slam him in the chest with my fist.

I'm so nervous and focused that I have completely forgotten about the body armor.

The sickening sound of my bones breaking is quickly followed by my scream. I try to club him with my other fist, but the pain is already radiating through my left arm and spreading. My last effort is a kick into the side of his knee, but the attempt is feeble, and I stumble back and fall on my butt.

Marek smiles but does not deliver one of his usual wisecracks. I realize why when he starts to walk. Being this high has weakened him considerably. He looks to be at about half his normal strength.

I devise a new strategy. I crawl over to where a giant rope is lying and wind my leg and arm through it. If I hold on with everything I have, I don't think he'll be strong enough to lift me.

Maybe I can wait until all his energy is gone.

He spits and snarls as he moves toward me, much more like a Level 3 than a cold-blooded killer. He looms over me, looking down at my swelling hand, and smiles.

Then he lifts his foot and stomps, grinding his heel into the back of my hand as I wail in agony.

Just as he's about to do it again, we both hear the elevator come to life.

I can tell by his expression that he has no idea who is coming. Neither do I.

I run through the possible scenarios. In my wildest dreams, it will be Natalie, Alex, or Grayson to rescue me once again. But there's no way they could know where I am. Then I remember Dr. H had said he was going to have past Omegas looking out for us and keeping an eye on Marek. Maybe, just maybe, it's one of them. But more than likely, it's one of Marek's many followers.

"One of us is about to be very happy," he says in a halting whisper, unsure of what to expect. Then he grins and grinds his heel into my hand one more time as I writhe in pain.

The elevator reaches the top, and we hear the cage door opening. When the figure reaches the doorway, my heart sinks. She's wearing the same yellow jacket and Yankees cap she had on the first time I saw her. It's the zombie who was watching us on our very first assignment.

Marek turns to me and grins. It's frightening because now virtually all his teeth have turned bright yellow and orange.

"Sorry," he says with a hoarse cackle. "One of mine."

He walks toward her as I try to devise a plan to fight the two of them. I'm drawing a blank. And then I hear it.

A scream.

It's Marek. He screams again as he backs away from her. She wastes no time and hits him with a flurry of kicks and punches. If she is weakened by the height, she doesn't show it.

Marek tries one last charge, but she levels him with a fully extended kick, right to the center of the chest. She powers into his body armor and pushes him backward.

Marek stumbles, and my final images of him are of his arms pinwheeling as he falls over the ledge and disappears, plunging toward the Hudson River sixty-five stories below.

Now the woman turns to me. I have no idea why she killed Marek—anyone that powerful has to have enemies—but I still assume I am next. I am too much of a loose end.

As she walks toward me, she staggers and I realize that she is weakening.

I have a chance.

I wrap my arm and leg around the rope as tightly as I can. I look up to see her looming above me. She is just a silhouette, but I can tell that she's studying me. The only sound is her shallow breathing as she tries to keep her strength.

She looks at my swollen hand, and I'm ready for her to crush it like Marek did. She doesn't. Instead, she kneels next to me and lifts it gently before placing it on my chest.

Then she looks at me, and the sunlight catches her face. Her cheeks are hollow and her skin is wrinkled and brown. Nothing about her looks human.

Except her eyes.

They still look the way they do in my memories. The way mine look when I check in the mirror.

One green, one blue.

Both very much alive.

She brushes the hair out of my face and looks down at me. Then she gently presses her lips against my forehead and holds them there for a few seconds.

My mind is racing. My life plays back in my head, and I question everything as I try to make sense of it all.

She doesn't talk. She just stands up and staggers to the elevator.

Finally, I'm able to gather the strength to speak. But as I do, the wind howls over me and I cannot be sure if she hears the single word I call out to her.

"Mom!"